POSSESSED
BY THE
VAMPIRE

KELLIE MCALLEN

COVER DESIGN BY

www.yocladesigns.com

CHAPTER ONE

"I'm going to tear your throat open and drain you dry!" Her attacker's harsh voice grated in her ear as one hand snaked around Caroline's waist, squeezing tight like a boa constrictor, and the other one clutched her throat, his nails pressing against her jugular. His hot breath puffed against her skin, meaning his fangs were only inches away from her.

She felt her pulse thudding against his grip as her heartbeat accelerated, and her heavy breathing blocked out all other sound. She instantly latched her sweaty palms over his hands.

"What are you going to do? Do you think you can stop me?" he hissed at her.

She closed her eyes for one brief moment, trying to remember what Roric had taught her. With a loud yell, she simultaneously rammed one foot down on top of his and shoved her elbow into his solar plexus. He grunted out in pain, and his body bowed. As soon as he loosened his grip, she whirled around with her hand extended like a blade and chopped him in the throat then kicked him in the calf.

He dropped to the ground, groaning and clutching his chest and leg as he rolled back and forth, his face pinched and red, obviously in pain. She gasped and fell to her knees on the ground beside him, her hands waving uselessly over him as she tried to figure out what to do.

"I'm sorry! I'm sorry! I didn't mean to hurt you!"

He let out a loud moan as his rocking slowed and his face gradually relaxed. He took one long, shuddering breath then opened his amber eyes and stared at her. "You are gonna pay for that."

He lunged for her, grabbing her arms and yanking her towards him. As soon as her body was on top of his, he flipped them over, pinning her underneath him. His arms caged her in, and his heavy body pressed down on hers, every inch touching. Their chests rose and fell in tandem as they traded gasping breaths.

She writhed under him, letting her legs fall open. His lower body slipped in between them till his pelvis was tight against hers. Every movement increased the friction. When a moan slipped from her throat, he grinned down at her and rubbed against her.

"You like that? Does that feel good?"

"Yes." The word wisped out on a breathy sigh.

Suddenly, his mouth descended. His lips claimed hers; his tongue swooped in to taste her. He ravaged her with his assault, taking and taking, never letting up till her breaths came fast and hard and gasping, till she couldn't breathe at all.

She shoved her hands against his chest, pushing him up, as she struggled to catch her breath. What was she doing? She was supposed to be fighting him off, not letting him molest her!

He leered down at her. "You did a good job. You're a lot stronger than I expected. I think you deserve a prize for winning that round."

She wanted that prize more than anything. Her body tingled as every nerve ending pulsed, crying out for attention. But there was no way she could take what he was offering.

It didn't stop her from grinding her center up against his hardness, though. "We don't have time. We have to leave in an hour."

He smiled and laughed. "Ha! You think I need an hour? I can be done in ten minutes."

She gave an exaggerated pout. "I thought it was supposed to be *my* prize."

His teasing tone disappeared, and his voice dropped an octave — low and husky. His golden eyes burned like flickering candlelight. "Oh, I'll make it good for you, baby. I promise."

Roric bent his head down to kiss her again, this time soft and sensual. He rested on his forearms, keeping his weight off her, but heat built up between them, making her whole body simmer. She let him explore her mouth — stroking her teeth, swirling his tongue around hers, sucking and nipping on her bottom lip.

Meanwhile, she pushed up his tee shirt and smoothed her hands over the firm, expansive planes of his back and sides. Feeling naughty, she shimmied her fingers under the waistband of his jeans and scratched at the round globes of his ass. He flexed under her fingers, tautening the muscles. She pressed down, pushing him into the crevice between her legs.

She didn't love him for his body, but she definitely

3

appreciated it. Like most born vampires, he was naturally big, but to stay in prime shape for his job as a VEA agent, Roric worked out. A lot. He was six feet, two inches, and 220 pounds of solid, bulging muscle.

He wanted Caroline to work out, too, starting with self-defense classes. It was part of the compromise they'd settled on. He'd try his best not to be bossy and overprotective, allowing her the chance to continue her support group for newly-turned vampires, as long as she was willing to let him teach her how to defend herself in case one of them got aggressive with her. He'd taught her strategies to get out of several different holds, and he tested her skills by randomly attacking her whenever she put herself in a vulnerable position.

It was nerve-wracking and frightening and exhilarating all at the same time whenever his hands wrapped around her body in a tight hold and growled threats in her ear. It made her panties wet most of the time.

He also made her spend an hour in the gym with him at least three times a week. That wasn't nearly as exciting, but she did enjoy watching his large, glistening muscles as he exercised, the bulges contracting with each flex.

But it was the bulge between his legs that he obviously wanted to exercise right now, and Caroline couldn't bring herself to resist, even though it was going to make them late. He'd gotten her all hot and bothered, and she needed some release.

"Let's move to the bed. I don't want you to be too sore," she said as soon as he gave her a chance to breathe again.

"You're the one who's going to be sore." He leapt to his feet, scooped her up in his arms, and tossed her onto the bed.   She giggled as she bounced on the navy damask comforter.

"You promise?"   Her center pulsed, anticipating the delicious soreness.

He pulled his shirt over his head and dropped it. "Baby, I'm going to make your nipples ache like my throat where you karate chopped me and your pussy throb with each heartbeat like my chest where you rammed your elbow.   Your legs will be too weak for you to walk.   We'll both be limping."

She sat up and reached for his waistband, unbuttoning his jeans.   His erection strained against the fabric and sprung free as soon as she pulled down the zipper.   "Are you going to assault me with your baton?"

"It's a deadly weapon.   Do you think you can handle it?"   He pushed his pants to the floor then stroked himself as he climbed up on the bed and knee-walked closer to her.

She nodded, grinning, then reached out and grabbed him.   He was hard and long and hot, his blood throbbing through the veins that encircled him.

"I like these pants.   They make your ass look sexy as hell.   But they have to go."   He grabbed the waistband of her leggings and pulled them down over her hips then yanked them off her feet and tossed them into the corner.

She fell back and spread her legs, presenting herself like a target.   Cool air brushed over her wet folds, but his hot gaze made them burn.

Her center pulsed, craving his touch.   But instead of touching her there, he shifted his gaze upwards, and his hands followed, sliding up her sides, pushing her shirt up. Her belly fluttered as he leaned down and kissed his way up to her breasts.

He didn't bother taking her shirt and bra off, just yanked the cups down, exposing her nipples. They stood up, pink and firm, anxious for his attention. He laid down with his legs between hers, his thigh pressing against her center, his upper body supported by one elbow. Then he latched onto one nipple, biting into it enough to draw blood then sucking it hard and deep into his mouth.

The pain was glorious. She closed her eyes, and her mouth fell open, a gasp escaping. Her body flexed upwards as he pulled on her. When he let go, she dropped back to the bed with a whimper. He laved her sore nipple with his tongue, the rough licks soothing and grating at the same time. When that nipple was aching, he switched to the other one.

When both nipples hurt so much she didn't know how she'd put her shirt back on, Roric finally pulled away from them and moved his attention farther down. Her wetness pressed against his leg, but he slid a hand between her folds to check, anyway. "Are you ready for me?"

"Oh God, Roric, if you make me wait another second, I'm going to use those moves you taught me to take you down and have my way with you."

"Umm, I might like that. You know strong women turn me on."

She smirked at that. It was true, but you'd never know it by the way he acted. Roric was first attracted to her because of the strength and bravery she showed when she fought back against the vampire who had infected her. But Roric was so desperate to keep her safe that he turned into an overbearing control freak whenever she did something the least bit dangerous.

Like usual, he didn't give her a chance to take the lead.

He liked being in control a little more than he liked a strong woman. He grabbed himself and slid into her. She sighed in pleasure as her body accepted him easily.

He stroked slow and gentle at first, but she was worked up and ready for more. She dug her nails into his back, pulling him down, and pushed her hips up to meet him. He took the hint and thrust into her harder and deeper. His biceps flexed on either side of her as he held himself over her, keeping the bulk of his weight off her as his hips pounded against hers. The pleasure built up with each stroke, filling her till she felt like she'd explode from the pressure.

"Don't stop," she begged, grabbing onto him tighter when his rhythm faltered.

His eyes pinched closed, and his face crumpled as he continued to stroke, slower and gentler. "I can't hold back much longer. I'm about to come."

Her muscles clenched against him, desperate for more friction. "Take me with you."

He started moving faster again, pistoning into her, his grunts matching her cries. She writhed under him, clutching at his sweat-slick body. With one final thrust, he roared and spilled inside her.

That last bit of friction was all she needed. Her orgasm slammed into her, and stars burst behind her eyelids as she squeezed her lids tight, trying to stop the world from spinning. She dug her fingers into Roric, holding on as her body exploded into a thousand pieces. Eventually, they all tumbled back to the bed. She lay in fragments, her bones disconnected from each other. She was unable to control any of them.

Slowly, reality crept back in. The stars disappeared,

and her senses returned. She could hear Roric breathing deeply, feel his hot flesh draped over her body, smell the masculine musk of his sweat. She hadn't drunk from him, but she didn't need to. She'd had him yesterday, and she'd probably take him again tomorrow.

Now that she'd moved in with him, and he'd made a big effort to spend more time with her, he was hers whenever she wanted him. They hadn't gone all the way yet, hadn't mated, but she thought she might be ready to.

Like regular people, they'd actually talked through their problems and were working on them together. It gave her hope that their relationship could survive. God knew they could barely survive without each other. They'd both been miserable when they were apart.

Roric might be a controlling vampire, but he would do anything to keep her safe. Caroline might have despised vampires in the past, but she loved this one. They were quite a pair.

Caroline lingered in her postcoital bliss for a long moment, relishing the feel of Roric's embrace and thinking about how she might tell him that she was ready to mate with him. She'd do it right now, but she wanted to make it special, and they didn't have time…

Her eyes popped open as she remembered they had somewhere important to be, and it wouldn't do to show up looking and smelling like they'd just had sex. She sat up, pushing Roric off of her.

"Roric, get up! We need to get ready!"

"Can't we just skip it? I'll be up for round two in a minute," he murmured into his pillow.

"No, we can't skip it! You're doing the introduction!"

CHAPTER TWO

Roric swerved into the full parking lot and squealed to a stop right in front of the entrance. He winced as he glanced at the clock. The event was supposed to start five minutes ago. Raven was going to be pissed, not to mention his father. Even when he was a model vampire, Roric never seemed to live up to his father's expectations, but lately he'd been breaking all the rules.

Caroline put her hand over his as he reached for the keys. "This is the fire lane, Roric. You can't park here."

"The closest spot is probably in the next town over. The entire vampire population is here." And they were all sitting inside, waiting for him.

"I'll find a spot. You go inside."

Roric nodded, smiling, and leaned over to kiss her. "Thanks. I'll find you afterwards."

He jumped out of the car, leaving his door open for Caroline, then dashed inside. The old building smelled strongly of fresh paint, and the white, cinderblock walls and new tile floors shined. Only a few people milled around the entry; most were already in the gymnasium.

Roric ignored them and dashed around to the back stage entrance, his slick, new dress shoes sliding as he ran.

When he slammed through the heavy door, everyone behind the curtain turned to gape at him. His father eyed his outfit, and Roric reached up instinctively to straighten his collar and tie. At least he looked okay, even if he did smell like sweat and sex since he didn't have time to shower. Caroline had persuaded him to go shopping with her and pick out a new suit. Since his old one was at least two sizes too small, he was sorely overdue for a new one.

"There you are! We were about to start without you." His father gave him a disapproving frown.

Raven glared at him. "You were supposed to be here half an hour ago!"

"I know, I'm sorry. I just got caught up in something." They could probably guess what had delayed him, based on his scent, but they were too tactful to mention it.

Roric would've been just as happy if they had started without him. He didn't see why he needed to introduce Raven, anyway. As head councilman, his father was going to emcee the event. He could easily say a few words about Raven. He'd been the one to hire her, after all.

Roric had been a little put off at first that his dad had brought her in without consulting him. He didn't think the Agency was any place for a prissy woman like Raven, and she'd been a pain in the butt, at first, wanting to play Good Cop with his suspects. But she'd been working hard to be an asset to the team and not a liability, and he had to admit her idea of a school to train new vampires was a good one.

Hopefully, it'd help to reduce the violent rogue activity that was plaguing Modesa and give Roric a little more free time to concentrate on other, more important things. Like

Caroline. Things were going great between them, and he intended to keep it that way.

"Are we ready?" his father asked, and Roric and Raven nodded.

He slipped through the slit in the stage curtain behind his father and scanned the crowd as he took his seat on the stage, looking for Caroline. Hundreds of vampires filled the gymnasium, but her long blonde hair and beautiful face stood out. His mouth stretched in a smile as soon as he spotted her, sitting with his brother and Ivy, like part of the family.

His father went to the podium to get things started. "Good evening ladies and gentlemen. I'm head councilman Kendar Asheron, and it's my pleasure to welcome you to the grand opening of the Vampire Training Academy."

A loud round of applause rose up from the crowd. His father waited for it to die down then continued his speech. "Today's world is much different from the one I grew up in. Vampires are no longer a creature of legend. We've been recognized by human society and are making great strides in gaining their acceptance. So much so, our population is exploding as more and more humans seek to join our ranks. Our hope is that this school will help prepare those new vampires to live peacefully with humans and vampires alike. Only then will we find true harmony with each other."

Roric was impressed with the way his father made it all sound so positive. He didn't say a word about the attacks that had led to so many new vampires or the uprising of rebel vampires who thought they were above the law. Another long round of applause made it obvious the crowd was impressed, too.

Roric didn't hate public speaking; he'd had to do it a few times in his role as head of the VEA. But his father was a born politician with a silver tongue. Following him made Roric feel like a tongue-tied Neanderthal. But all Roric had to do tonight was introduce Raven, so it wasn't too bad.

After the applause died down, he swapped places with his father. The applause didn't follow him. Instead, the crowd stared at him like they weren't sure what he was doing up there. He gritted his teeth and resisted the urge to pull at his collar, but he did take a quick peek down to make sure his tie was straight and his fly wasn't open.

Then he focused his gaze on Caroline. Looking at her always brought a smile to his face and calmed his nerves. She grinned back at him, a wide, knowing smile followed by a wink that put dirty thoughts in his mind. She'd given him that age-old public speaking advice earlier, to imagine the audience in their underwear, so of course, all he could think about was her wearing nothing but sexy lingerie. He swallowed hard and prayed he didn't get an erection.

"Hello, everyone. My name is Roric Asheron, and I'm the head of the Vampire Enforcement Agency. It's been my pleasure to have Raven Lorenzo on the team these last few months. She's been an invaluable asset, helping us interview and counsel the vampires who end up at the Agency. They like talking to her a lot better than me." That got a small chuckle from the crowd and made Roric feel a little more comfortable.

"Because of her own experience being changed as a young teen and adopted into a loving vampire family, Raven has a real heart for newly-turned vampires. She's worked tirelessly on the creation of this school, and we're thrilled to see it come to fruition. Please give a warm welcome to Miss Raven Lorenzo."

The audience clapped loudly again, more for Raven than for him, he was sure, as she took over the podium. Roric went to sit behind her in the chair next to his father, wishing he could go sit next to Caroline instead.

Raven spoke eloquently for several minutes about the goals of the school. He knew that many of the vampires who'd be sent there weren't going to be happy about it, but she talked it up like it would be a wonderful experience for them. She made it sound so good, he almost believed her.

But the truth was, they still had an uphill battle in front of them. Those who'd been turned against their will wouldn't be eager to be separated from their friends and family while they completed the three-month program, and the rogues who thought being a vampire meant doing whatever you wanted would be downright hostile to any form of authority.

Raven wisely avoided any mention of enrollment requirements. The council had already made an official announcement about it that had created an uproar, so everyone knew the score. All vamps less than three months turned would be required to attend, along with any unregister vampires, and any vampire caught breaking the law would also go through a rehabilitation course as part of their sentence.

Roric was glad he wasn't in charge of the school. He wasn't sure Raven was going to be able to handle it, either, but she'd hired several other strong vampires who'd hopefully help her keep things under control.

Raven finished her speech and told the audience to feel

free to explore the school and help themselves to the refreshments. Roric stood up as soon as she finished, eager to get back to Caroline, but Raven hustled after him, her high heels clicking loudly on the wooden stage.

"Roric, can I talk to you for a minute?"

He slipped behind the curtain before turning towards her with a sigh. Didn't she want to get out there to chat with people? "Yeah?"

"I don't know what's up with you lately. You've been taking a lot of days off, and when you are there, it's like your head is in the clouds. Maybe you don't care about this school, but this is a big deal to me and our community. This school is going to need the full support of the Agency."

"Look, Raven. I'm sorry I was late. I appreciate the importance of the school, I do. And the Agency will be there to support you. But I'm not married to my job anymore. Caroline is my number one priority now, not work."

Raven sneered and flicked her hair back. Of course, she didn't much like that. She was in love with the job and thought everybody else should be, too. Plus, he had a feeling she was a little jealous. He thought she might be attracted to him, the way she acted sometimes.

If he was honest, Raven made a lot more sense as a partner for him. She didn't have any hangups about being a vampire. She came from a respectable vampire family much like his. She worked side by side with him at the Agency. And he had to admit she was beautiful with her sleek, black bob and classy, form-fitted business suits.

But Roric had fallen for Caroline the minute he laid eyes on her, and he'd been a goner ever since, despite the fact that she'd hated vampires and resented him for turning her into one, even though he was only trying to save her life. She'd gotten over it, though, and by some miracle she'd fallen for him, too, even though he was the antithesis of what she thought she wanted in a mate.

He couldn't change the fact that he was a vampire, but he was trying hard to be the kind of man she deserved — one who put her first, treated her with respect, and didn't try to control her. It went against his natural inclinations, but he was working on it. Thank God she forgave him when he screwed things up and was willing to give him another chance, because he didn't know how he could live without her.

He fully intended to make her his mate as soon as she let him. He wished they were already mated so she could've been next to him on the stage instead of out in the crowd somewhere. He was anxious to get to her now and hoping Raven would drop the issue.

Of course, that wasn't in her nature. Raven was just as stubborn as he was. She put her hands on her slim waist and glared at him. "How can anything be more important than your job right now, Roric? If you haven't noticed, we're in the middle of a crisis, and you're the leader of the Agency. If we don't get these new vampires under control, the humans are going to take matters into their own hands and wage war against us."

He scowled at her and loosened his tie. "Believe me, I get that. And I'm doing my damnedest to stay on top of it. I work my ass off 60 hours a week. But I'm not taking the fate of the entire vampire race on my shoulders. I want to have a life that's worth fighting for."

He stomped off, not willing to listen to any more of her

condemnation. If he was being honest, her words hit a little too close to home. Was she right? Was he being selfish by devoting so much time to his relationship when the vampire world was in a state of emergency? Yes, he was the leader of the Agency, but did that mean he had to forfeit his personal life?

CHAPTER THREE

"Can we ditch this scene and head to the bar now?" Taven threw back his cup of punch like a shot of liquor and scowled at the crowd in the large gymnasium. Knowing him, it wouldn't have surprised Caroline if he'd poured vodka in it from a flask hidden in his suit coat.

"It's only been five minutes since the welcome speech. Don't you think you should mingle a little bit, as a show of support?" Caroline sipped at her own punch and nibbled on a cookie, wondering where Roric was.

She still felt out of place in a room full of vampires, even though she was one. A couple hundred voices echoed off the cinderblock walls and polished wood floors, setting her teeth on edge, and even cold-skinned vampires could heat up a room if you crammed enough of them in there. Caroline fanned herself ineffectively with her tiny clutch.

Of course, as soon as Roric showed up, he was much more likely to want to mingle with the guests than his brother, and he'd want Caroline to go with him. He might even want to introduce her to everyone as his girlfriend. That made her even more nervous.

Would people ask questions she didn't want to answer? Would they think she wasn't good enough for Roric? She was a poor bartender who'd only been a vampire for a few months, and Roric was a well-known born vampire from the most prestigious vampire family in town. They were bound to judge her and find her lacking.

She tugged on the tight, black, designer dress Roric had bought for her — the most expensive piece of clothing she'd ever owned — wondering if she looked as out of place as she felt, like a child playing dress-up in her mother's clothes. Maybe she should just hang out here with Taven and Ivy, instead.

A hand snaked around her waist, and Caroline automatically tensed and sucked in a breath, ready for a fight. Roric leaned over her shoulder and whispered in her ear.

"Relax, babe. It's just me. I won't attack you here. Although I'm impressed with your reflexes. All that training is paying off. I like what it's doing to your ass, too." He slid a hand in between them and squeezed her butt cheek. Caroline blushed, wondering if anyone could see where his hand was.

He put his hands on her waist as she turned towards him, and she stroked a hand down the starched fabric of his dress shirt. "You did a great job on your speech. And you look nice in your new suit."

Roric made a face and glanced between her, his brother, and Ivy. "You don't think I sounded like a numbskull compared to my father and Raven?"

Caroline wrinkled her brow. Did Roric really feel that way about himself? He of all people should feel confident in this crowd. The fact that he didn't made her feel marginally better about her own insecurity. "Of course not. You have a very commanding presence. You sounded like the leader you are."

"Yeah, bro. You sounded just like a politician. I didn't believe a word you said." Taven smirked then crumpled his cup and tossed it towards the trash.

"Speaking of, I should go rub shoulders with some people. Come on, I want to introduce you while we're here." Roric let go of her waist and reached for her hand.

Caroline grimaced. "Do you think that's a good idea? I'm not sure I fit in here."

He smiled and glanced down at her cleavage. "Of course you do. You're the most beautiful woman here. Come on, I want to go show you off."

Ivy turned towards Taven with her hands on her hips. "Are you going to go rub shoulders and show me off?"

Ivy didn't fit in any better than Caroline did. She was an orphan, a former prostitute who currently waitressed at a diner, and Taven had turned her illegally around the same time that Caroline had been turned. But unlike Caroline, Ivy liked attention and seemed totally at ease. Caroline wished she had half her confidence.

Taven stroked his hand down Ivy's snug, red dress. "No way, babe. I'm keeping you all to myself. Otherwise, one of these suits might try to steal you from me."

Caroline stared longingly at her and Taven, wishing she could trade places for the night. Roric tugged Caroline away from them and led her towards a group of distinguished-looking men. Her stomach twisted, and a cold sweat broke out on her forehead. She put a hand to her head and dug her high heels into the floor.

"Roric, are those council members? What are you

going to say to them?"

He stopped and turned towards her. "Yeah, I need to say hello, at least. And I'm going to introduce you as the woman I love."

He didn't say it, but she could feel his unspoken desire. He gave her that intense look that made her made her feel like her insides were molten lava, and she realized nothing would make her, or him, happier. She loved him, and she couldn't imagine that would ever change. What was she waiting for?

"You could tell them I'm the woman you're going to mate, instead. If you wanted to," she whispered.

Intense emotions flashed across Roric's face for a moment, then he grabbed her and lifted her off her feet and swung her around in a circle. Everyone around them turned and gaped at them.

Caroline squealed and pounded him on the shoulders. "Put me down! You're making a scene!"

He slowed to a stop and let her body slide down his till her feet were on the floor again. Then his voice boomed out. "Don't mind us. We're just celebrating our engagement."

The crowd smiled and clapped, and several people headed towards them to congratulate them. The next half hour was a blur of names and faces as Roric introduced her to everyone he knew. Caroline shook hands, smiled, and said hello to everyone, but she was so overwhelmed she knew she wouldn't remember a single one of them.

Everyone acted very happy for them, and there were too many people wanting to talk to them for anyone to have a chance to ask the questions Caroline was dreading, like who her family was, what she did for a living, or how she and Roric had met. They'd probably start wondering where she came from eventually, but for now, they just accepted that she was worthy of him.

When the crowd cleared a bit, Roric's father came over. Because he'd stopped aging in his twenties, he looked like a wizened version of Roric and Taven with short, dark hair and broad shoulders. Only he looked a lot more at ease in a suit than they did. His genteel voice and graceful movements spoke of a life in politics, not law enforcement. "Well, son, this is quite a surprise. Didn't you just meet? Caroline, is it?"

"Caroline has been living with me for a few months, Dad."

She and his father had met before, of course. She was living in the same house as him. But it was a sprawling mansion with several wings, and she and Roric kept mostly to Roric's suite, so she didn't cross paths very often with his father. He was still practically a stranger to her.

"Well, yes, of course. But I didn't realize you intended to mate with her."

Roric wrapped his arm around her, pulling her into his side. "I love her. She's the one."

Kendar put a finger to his lip, and his eyes focused off into the distance, or maybe the past. "Hmm, yes, I remember that feeling. Caroline, you were just recently turned, weren't you?"

Roric scowled at him and tensed against her. He held a lot of animosity towards his father for pushing his mother to become a vampire so she could mate with him, and he blamed his father for his mother's eventual suicide. Roric had always vowed he would never ask a human to change for him.

Kendar had no idea that Roric had been the one to change her, and without her permission. If he did, he'd really be surprised by their engagement.

Caroline stroked his chest, trying to soothe the worries she was sure his father's words were evoking. "Yes, and Roric has helped make the transition very easy for me. I'm lucky to have him. Your son is a wonderful man; you should be proud of him. And I'm honored to become part of your family."

Kendar raised his eyebrows at that, and he gave a small smile. He took her hand and covered it with his own. "Well, welcome to the family, Caroline. I hope you and my son make each other very happy."

He walked away then, and Caroline and Roric both let out long breaths then turned to each other and chuckled. Then Roric's face softened. "Thank you for that. It means a lot to me."

"For what? Telling your father how I feel about you? It was the truth, you know."

Roric pulled her into him and kissed her, mindless of the crowd around them. She blocked them out and let herself enjoy the moment. She was going to be mated! Never in a million years did she imagine that she'd fall in love and mate with a vampire, but she couldn't bring herself to regret any of the events that had led her to that moment.

There were only two people in the crowd who didn't seem happy about the announcement. When they pulled apart, Raven stood nearby trying to hide a look of disdain. She flicked her head, making her sleek hair swing backwards then fall right back into place, then she pulled on her cropped suit jacket and stalked towards them.

"Congratulations." She held out a stiff hand, shook hands with them, then stalked off without saying anything else. Caroline glanced at Roric and raised an eyebrow.

"Don't worry about her. She's just thinks I should be married to my job." He grinned at her and tried to play it off, but Caroline had a suspicion that Raven wanted Roric. Caroline still worried sometimes about how much time Roric and Raven spent together at the office, but Roric had asked Caroline to mate with him, not Raven, so if there was attraction, hopefully it was one-sided.

After she left, Taven and Ivy came up to them. Taven slugged Roric in the shoulder then put an arm around him in a manly hug. "Congratulations, bro. Better you than me. When are you snapping on the old ball and chain?"

Caroline winced and glanced at Ivy whose face crumpled at Taven's comment. Ivy desperately wanted Taven to make that kind of commitment to her, but Taven was a lot more reluctant than his brother. It was about the only thing he wasn't in competition with his brother about.

Roric saw Ivy's pained look, too, and tried to make it better. "Ah, I see the way you look at Ivy. You won't be far behind me."

Taven made a face at Roric. "I think I'll keep my freedom for a little while. We've only been dating a couple months. We're immortal; it's not like there's a big hurry."

"Yeah, well, I don't want to waste another minute of our eternity." Roric turned towards Caroline and gave her that look again. Roric was the one acting soft, but she melted like a marshmallow.

Taven rolled his eyes and made a gagging noise. "I don't want to waste another minute at this lame party. You all ready to hit the bar?"

Roric glanced around at the crowd of people. The place was still packed. Would he want to stay till most of them were gone? Caroline hoped not.

"Yeah, I suppose we could get out of here now. I've talked to everyone important. Caroline, are you ready to go?"

Caroline nodded, eager to get out of there and out of the spotlight. Her feet hurt from standing in high heels, and she wanted to go home, take off her tight dress, and continue where she and Roric left off. There was supposed to be an afterparty at the bar where she worked, but she had a feeling that Roric wouldn't want to stay there any longer than she did.

They made their way towards the exit, but their path was slowed since everyone they passed had something to say to Roric, either congratulations about the engagement, or questions about the school, or complaints about what the Agency was or wasn't doing about the rogues. Roric was polite and friendly but he kept his responses brief and didn't stop walking. Caroline was impressed with how smoothly he handled them all. He really was the poster boy for the modern vampire. She couldn't have picked a better one if she'd tried.

Of course, they didn't know his secret — that he'd broken the biggest law by turning a human. If they did, his fall from grace would be swift and dramatic. But only a handful of people knew the truth, and none of them had anything to gain by turning him in.

"Roric! Good to see you, man!" A preppy-looking vampire about the same age as Roric approached them with a wide smile and his hand out to shake. Of course, it was hard to tell how old vampires were since born vampires stopped aging in their early twenties and turned vampires stayed whatever age they were when they were changed.

"Savon, how are you?" Roric gave him a big smile in return and shook the man's hand like they were old friends, but the way he squeezed Caroline's hand told her he wasn't as happy to see the guy as he pretended.

"Good, good. Working on my master's at Princeton. I just came back for the grand opening. Glad things are going so well for you. Your old dad put you in charge of the Agency. Must be nice to have that kind of privilege. Now you're getting mated. Last I knew, you'd had one date with just about every vampire in Modesa, but never a second one. I didn't think you'd ever find someone. How'd you score this one? She looks like she's out of your league. Did your dad bring her in from out of town for you?"

The guy's eyed roved up and down her body, and Caroline's mouth fell open. What a jerk! Caroline wanted to smack him, but she couldn't do that, so instead she blurted out the first thing that came to mind, trying to make Roric look good.

"I was attacked by a rogue vampire, and Roric rescued me." As soon as the words left her mouth, Roric tensed, and Caroline worried that she'd made a big mistake. Did born vampires look down on turned ones? Would her human past bring down Roric's status?

Savon gawked at her, and so did everyone else around them. Suddenly, they all started talking. Caroline winced, but then their words filtered through her anxiety.

"What a hero!"

"How romantic!"

"What a great story!"

Roric wrapped his arm around her waist and squeezed her close to him as he blushed and murmured in response to the compliments. Caroline sighed in relief and gave a wobbly smile. Thank God they seemed to be impressed by his heroics.

Savon scurried off, looking defeated, and the crowd eventually dispersed, allowing Roric and Caroline to make it to the door. Roric pushed the door open, letting in a blast of cool, night air that instantly soothed Caroline's overheated body.

They were halfway out the door when a loud blast deafened them, and a strong pressure hit them like a wave, knocking them to the ground. Several hundred screams rose up behind them.

CHAPTER FOUR

A flash of white light surrounded Roric like someone had opened up the door to heaven, but the intense heat that seared his flesh felt more like hell. So did the pain that pierced through his head like ice picks rammed in both ears. It smelled like hell, too. The bitter charcoal scent of gunpowder mixed with the acrid scent of blood and burnt flesh. Was he dead?

Roric choked and gagged on the thick cloud of smoke as his lungs gasped for air. His heart thundered in his chest, making his whole body throb. He wouldn't feel his heartbeat if he was dead, would he?

He'd never imagined his own death before, never given it much thought at all. Vampires lived forever as long as they avoided the sun and fed the beast that roared inside them, demanding blood. Roric assumed he would live as long as he wanted to. He never considered the possibility that someone else might want him dead.

He was blinded by the light and deafened by the ringing in his ears, so he groped at the space around him, trying to figure out where he was. His hands landed on something soft and curved. Caroline!

She moved underneath his touch, and her hands scrambled to find his. She laced her trembling fingers between his, but Roric wasn't satisfied with that. He tugged his hand from hers and pulled her into his arms, wrapping their bodies together. She was alive, and that was all that mattered.

The vampire healing ability meant they'd both be fine eventually. They held each other for a long moment as their bodies recovered. Slowly, Roric's sight started to return, the white light dimming to gray, and the ringing in his ears quieted until he could hear the chaos around them. Caroline's face materialized before him, whole and unharmed. He reached out to stroke her cheek.

"Are you okay?" The words rasped out of his soot-filled throat.

"I'm fine. Are you hurt?" Her face pinched with worry.

"No, I'm good." Thank God they were so far away from the blast.

A siren wail rose up in the distance then quickly grew louder. Moments later, the first emergency responders burst through the doors. They stared, dumbstruck, by the overwhelming sight.

A cloud of dust still hung in the air, making it hard to see, but what Roric could make out was horrendous. A thick layer of bloody dust and rubble covered the floor — mangled chairs, chunks of cinderblock, wood from the stage. Bodies and body parts lay strewn amongst the debris in various states of injury.

Roric climbed to his feet, pulling Caroline with him, then turned towards the EMTs. "Listen, all these people are vampires. Most of their injuries will heal without any medical care. For those who've lost limbs, if they're put back together properly and secured in place, their body parts will reattach and heal. They may need help finding them, though."

One of the EMTs glanced down at a detached foot lying nearby and gingerly picked it up. It wasn't the only body part in sight. Roric could only assume that many vampires had been blown to smithereens by the blast. There was no saving them. How many lives had been lost? His heart burned with anguish like it'd been dipped in acid.

The only thing that kept him from having a mental breakdown was the fact that he knew Caroline was alive. What if he had lost her? He couldn't bear to think about it. But what about his family? His father? Taven? Ivy? His eyes scanned the room frantically, but it was too chaotic to make out much of anything.

He pulled out his cell phone, but there were no missed called or text messages. He jabbed at his brother's contact. The phone rang several times, and Roric tried to listen for the sound in the crowd, but there was too much commotion to pick it out. It might not even be ringing. Taven probably turned the sound off for the speeches.

Eventually, the call went to voice mail. Roric barked out an anxious message. "Taven, where are you ? Are you okay?"

As soon as he hung up, he sent a quick text, hoping his brother would try to reach him, too, and would see it.

He turned towards Caroline and stroked her cheek to reassure himself that she was all right. "Caroline, I have to go find Dad and Taven."

She took his hand and nodded. "I'll help you look for

them."

They shuffled through the rubble, looking for familiar faces, but it was hard to make much progress. The less-injured vampires were getting up and moving around, looking for limbs or loved ones. The more severely-injured begged for assistance, grabbing onto them as they passed by.

Roric weaved through the crowd as quickly as he could, looking for Taven. He saw Raven and several of his other agents, but he couldn't see his brother anywhere, nor Ivy. He kept checking his phone, but there was nothing. The longer they looked, the less crowded the room got as those who could cleared out. Roric's heartbeat sped up as his eyes flitted around the room, not seeing any sign of any of them. Where was his family?

"Roric, look." Caroline grabbed ahold of his arm. Roric whipped his head around and followed her pointing finger.

His father lay in a corner, awake and alive, but obviously in distress. Roric rushed over to him, shoving his way through the crowd and bounding over bodies.

"Dad, are you okay?" He knelt down beside his father whose face was red and twisted in agony.

"Roric." His father croaked out a weak reply.

Roric's hands and eyes roved down the length of his father's body, looking for the source of his pain. The limbs were all attached, but his left foot was twisted around backwards. Roric grabbed the hem of his father's pants leg and ripped open the fabric to mid-thigh with one tug. One of the bones was broken and gouging through the skin.

"Oh shit. We have to get this back in place before it heals like this. It'll be worse if we wait. I'm going to reset the bone, Dad. It's gonna hurt like hell. Are you ready?"

His father winced and moaned. Roric's tense face softened as Caroline took his father's hand in hers. "You can squeeze my hand if you want to, sir."

Roric carefully lifted his father's calf. "On three, okay?"

His father clasped onto Caroline's hand and tensed his muscles. Roric braced himself, moved his hands into position, then started counting. "One, two, three!"

On three, he yanked his father's leg till his foot was straight again. His father screamed out in agony then slumped against the wall, lifeless. Roric leapt up and knelt by his head. "Dad, are you okay?"

His father groaned and rolled his head towards Roric. His eyelids fluttered open, and he opened and closed his mouth a few times before he mumbled out a thank you.

"Caroline, get one of the EMTs to bring a stretcher. He needs to go to the hospital for an x-ray to make sure the bones are in the right place."

Caroline jumped up and scurried off. Roric stayed and stroked his dad's face with one hand and squeezed his shoulder with the other. "You're all right, Dad. You're going to be okay."

"Is your brother okay?" his dad whispered.

Roric clenched his jaw and swallowed hard as his anxiety came rushing back again. "I'm not sure. I haven't found him yet."

The EMTs dropped a stretcher down beside him then and started assessing Kendar's injuries. Roric explained what he'd done. They agreed to take his father to the hospital.

"Don't worry about me. Go find your brother," his

father mumbled as the EMTs lifted the stretcher.

"Okay, Dad. We'll come check on you as soon as I find him." He prayed he could keep that promise, but he was losing hope that he'd ever find Taven. He'd seen no sign of him yet, which probably meant there was nothing left to find. He wasn't ready to accept that yet, though, so as soon as they carried his father off, he started scanning the room again.

Most of the people had cleared out. He worked systematically around the room, examining each person, ruling them out one by one. Too short, too thin, too blonde, too female. None of them were Taven or Ivy. He headed towards the side of the room, intent on looking at each face. Caroline scurried after him, but she didn't question him.

Roric grabbed ahold of each person he saw and yanked them around till he could look them in the eye. When it was obvious they weren't his brother, he asked each one of them, "Have you seen Taven Asheron?"

They all answered no, not since the blast.

Eventually, Roric dropped his eyes to the ground and started searching the rubble, trying to remember what kind of shoes his brother was wearing, what color suit. Most of the severed body parts that littered the floor earlier had been claimed. Roric picked up each of the remaining parts and examined them, mindless of the gruesomeness. Would Taven have worn wingtips? Were Ivy's nails painted?

Roric's heart seized in his chest, the throbbing, aching muscle tightening till it could barely beat, as he held a thumb in his hand, turning it over and over, trying to picture what his brother's fingers looked like. Why couldn't he remember? He'd known his brother for twenty-one years. Shouldn't he be able to recognize his thumbnail?

He was so caught up in his angst, he didn't hear Caroline calling his name till she grabbed his chin and turned his face towards the doorway. His heart suddenly took off again, a propeller about to explode through his chest wall.

"Taven!" He raced towards the door, leaping over anything in between them.

Taven stood in the doorway with Ivy, looking stunned and untouched. His suit was still clean, only the tiniest bit of dust from the air settling on his shoulders. Roric slammed into his brother, grabbing him in a hug that sent them spinning them around in a circle. Taven eventually dug his heels into the floor and shoved his hands against Roric's chest, pushing him away.

Roric grabbed onto his brother's shoulders to steady himself. Her felt lightheaded and dizzy, and the room was whirling. "You're alive! Thank God! Where were you? I've been looking all over for you?"

Taven looked around the room as he talked, gawking at the devastation. "We left while you were talking to that douche bag, Savon. We've been at the Taproom, waiting for everyone to show up. Then there was a special report on the TV about an explosion. We came back as soon as we heard about it. Is Dad okay?"

"He broke his leg, but he'll be all right. They took him to the hospital already."

Taven nodded, hiding his relief behind a stoic mask and running a hand nervously through his hair, mussing the gelled strands till they looked the way he normally wore them, finger-styled and messy. "Do you think this was the work of rogue vampires or humans?"

Roric looked around, still overwhelmed and appalled by the tragedy. How could anyone care so little about life, regardless of whether it was human or vampire? "We made an easy target for any human who had it out for vampires, but it doesn't make sense for them to destroy the school. Rogues, on the other hand, have plenty of motivation. This school represents everything they're against, and they consider all the vampires in support of it just as much of an opposition to their goals as humans, if not more so."

Roric wanted to kick himself for not suggesting more security for the event. Vampires didn't worry too much about that kind of stuff since they were immortal, but none of them had anticipated a bomb.

"This is going to be a setback, but they didn't do as much damage as they could've. At least the school's still standing. It looks like most of the damage is contained to the gym."

Roric shook his head. "That's good, but there were hundreds of vampires here. The loss of life has to be enormous."

"I don't know. Have you seen the crowd outside? There are hundreds of vamps out there who made it out okay. The police are questioning them." Taven jabbed a thumb towards the doors.

"Really?" Roric pushed past Taven and headed outside. He sucked in a deep breath as the cool, clean, night air hit him then coughed up a glob of dusty phlegm and spit it on the ground.

Sure enough, police had the area cordoned off, their cruisers making a circle around the front of the school, their headlights brightening the scene. It wouldn't do much to contain a vampire who wanted to leave, but most were standing around, shell-shocked. Dozens of officers were questioning them. The vampires seemed willing to share their version of events.

Roric desperately wanted to go home, fall into bed with Caroline, and try to block out the whole experience, but he knew his night was far from over. He needed to switch over from victim to investigator mode and collect whatever information he could while the scene was still fresh.

He glanced over to Caroline who was holding onto Ivy. "Caroline, Taven and I have got work to do. Why don't you and Ivy take one of our cruisers and go home? We're probably going to be here a while."

Caroline opened her mouth. He knew she wanted to argue, but there was nothing she could say that would change his mind, and she knew it, too. But she still asked, "Isn't there something we can do to help?"

She didn't have any medical training to help the victims, and besides, there were very few injuries to be treated. Most of the vamps were healing just fine on their own. She wasn't an agent, so she couldn't question the witnesses, either.

"No, babe. And I'll feel better if I know you're safe at home." He felt nervous, like the night still held the threat of danger. He was probably going to feel that way for a long time. Hopefully Caroline would forgive him if he acted a little overprotective for a while.

"Okay, well, be safe, okay? There's something I want to do with you later." She winked at him and ran a finger down his chest. His dick stirred at her words, remembering that she'd agreed to mate with him. It wouldn't happen tonight, not after all this, but the promise buoyed his spirits and gave him the energy he needed to push through the rest of the night.

He pulled her close and kissed her, savoring the feel of her small, soft body pressed against his. He couldn't wait to bury himself inside her and make her his forever. She pushed him away with a wicked smile when his dick got hard between them. "I'll see you at home."

Ivy gave Taven a kiss, too, then the girls took Taven's keys and headed off towards his cruiser. Roric watched them as they walked away, not willing to take his eye off Caroline until she was safely in the car.

His gaze hardened when he noticed someone else watching them — a man with buzzed hair wearing a wife beater that showed off arms full of prison tattoos. He'd brought in the rogue before but didn't have enough evidence to charge him. The vamp looked down at his phone once the girls were in the car and tapped on it. Roric stalked towards him, his mind flicking through the questions he intended to ask him.

CHAPTER FIVE

"What are you doing here, Derrick?" Roric pinned his eyes on the known rogue standing under the parking light and shoved through the crowd. Surprisingly, the rogue didn't take off like Roric expected him to.

Instead, his lips curled in a malevolent smile, revealing a crooked row of stained teeth that looked yellow under the glow of the parking lot. The light reflected off his greasy skin and emphasized the purple hollows under his eyes. "It's a public event, isn't it? I have every right to be here."

"No, it was by invite only, actually. And I'm pretty sure you didn't get one."

That had been their only attempt at attendance control. The gym wasn't big enough for more than a couple hundred guests, max, so they'd sent out invitations to the vampires most likely to make contributions to the school. Roric thought they'd be checking invitations at the door, but no one had asked for his. Of course, he was late, and recognizable, so maybe they just didn't bother with him.

"So, the highfalutin vamps get invited to the party, but the vamps like me are the ones who'll get forced to enroll."

Derrick pulled a pack of cigarettes out of the back pocket of his grungy jeans, making Roric flinch at the sudden movement.

"I don't know, has it been less than three months since you were registered?" Roric glared at him knowingly. He'd been the one to force Derrick to register when he'd brought him in for suspicious behavior.

"Just past. Too bad. Guess I won't be spending much time at your fancy school, after all." Derrick snapped his fingers and gave an aw-shucks expression that quickly morphed back into an evil scowl. Then he dug a cigarette out of the pack, stuck it between his lips, and flicked open a lighter.

If anyone needed training in how to be a law-abiding vampire, it was vamps like Derrick, but Roric doubted the school would've done Derrick any good, anyway. He had no intention of following the laws. Roric's body vibrated with frustration, wishing he had an excuse to arrest him. His hands automatically reached for his weapons, but he wasn't wearing his holster.

"So there was no reason for you to come to the party, then. You should be grateful you weren't invited. You could have been one of the victims who didn't make it out."

"Oh, I had a reason to be here. I had a delivery to make. But I wasn't worried about my safety. I made sure I wasn't in there when the blast went off." Derrick took a puff on his cigarette and blew the smoke in Roric's face. When the smoke dissipated, he was looking at Roric with eager expectation.

Roric narrowed his eyes and stared at him. He might as well have come right out and said he planted the bomb! Was he that stupid that he'd brag about that to a VEA agent? Or did he want to be a suspect? Either way, Roric was happy to toss him in a cell till they got to the bottom of it. Any night that Derrick spent in jail was a night he wasn't out causing trouble.

Roric tensed, unsure what to do. Derrick's admission was suspicious enough to warrant bringing him in, but he didn't have a weapon or even handcuffs. If Derrick had any brain cells at all, he'd run as soon as Roric made a move. That was debatable, but Roric didn't want to miss his chance.

He flicked his eyes around the scene, looking for Taven. His brother was nearby, questioning another witness. He sensed Roric's eyes on him, though, and glanced his way. Roric glared at him then flicked his eyes towards Derrick, trying to get Taven's attention without making Derrick suspicious.

Thank God, Taven knew him well enough to read his expression. Taven quickly abandoned his witness and swept in behind Derrick. Roric repeated Derrick's words so there'd be no question what he wanted from his brother.

"So, you're saying you delivered something to the party, and you knew there would be an explosion?"

Taven's eyes bugged out, and he reached for his missing weapons, too. Roric lunged for Derrick from the front, and Taven grabbed him from behind, pinning him in between them. Derrick jerked, but there was nowhere for him to go.

"You are one stupid son of a bitch, Derrick. But thanks for making this easy on us." Roric hauled him over to his cruiser with Taven's help and tossed him in the backseat.

Roric was eager to take him to the station and question

him some more, but he was hesitant to leave the scene. The human police had jumped in since there was no proof that this was a vampire crime, and Roric was happy to have them since the Agency wasn't equipped to process a bomb scene. But he wanted a chance to question the witnesses. They might tell him things they wouldn't tell the humans.

Roric glanced around to see if anyone had noticed him taking Derrick into custody. The last thing he wanted was for the police to take his witness from him, but no one seemed to be paying any attention to him. He decided it wouldn't kill Derrick to simmer in the cruiser for a while. Roric stuck his phone up against the back window and snapped a picture of Derrick when he looked up. Then he headed off to do some questioning.

He asked everyone the same basic questions — did they see anything suspicious or anyone who looked out of place, and did they recognize the man in the photo. Derrick obviously wasn't dressed to blend in, even as a delivery person, but no one had any recollection of seeing him. After getting the same answers from everyone, Roric went over to the supervising police officer to compare notes.

"Hey man, anyone telling you anything useful?"

Thankfully, Officer Castille knew him and was willing to talk to him. The middle-aged man with sagging jowls, a pot belly straining his dark blue uniform, and a headful of gray hair gave his signature sigh. "No, no one saw anything. But it's no surprise. Based on the blast pattern, my guess is the bomb was backstage. The perp could've easily snuck in, set the bomb, and slipped out of there without anyone seeing him."

Roric scowled. It would help a lot if someone had seen Derrick inside. He was talking smack, but unless he

40

actually confessed, they couldn't charge him without any evidence.

"Okay, well, let me know if you hear anything, will ya?" Roric wasn't as willing to share info as Castille was, so he left it at that. If he couldn't pin it on Derrick, he'd pass him on to Castille's team, but he wanted his shot first.

Roric saw Taven walk away from a witness, so he hustled over to talk to him before he started another interview. "Hey bro, got anything yet?"

Taven puffed up his cheeks and blew out an exasperated breath. "Nope. nothing. These people have their heads so far up their asses, they wouldn't have noticed anything suspicious if the perp had asked them to hold the bomb while he tied his shoelaces."

"I don't think there was anything suspicious for them to see. Castille thinks the bomb was placed backstage."

Taven scowled at him and pounded his fist into his palm. "Shit. Why didn't we have security in place? That was a dumb ass mistake."

Roric wasn't in charge of the event, Raven was, but he still couldn't help but blame himself for not anticipating problems. Raven didn't know any better, but he did. The school was a huge deal, and putting on a grand opening celebration was like slapping a big target on it.

He should've been more proactive. It was his job to protect the people of Modesa. A simple security check at the door might've kept out the perp. One agent on duty. How many lives would've been spared?

But no, he'd been too preoccupied with Caroline to give the party more than a passing thought. He'd spent more time preparing his introduction and picking out a new suit than he had thinking about the potential for danger.

Guilt weighed on him, crushing him.

There was nothing he could do to reverse the damage, but he'd do everything he could to nail the perp who did this and bring the victims some justice. He had a suspect already. All he had to do was prove he'd done it.

"I'm taking the suspect to the station to interrogate him. You wanna come?" Taven was a good partner when it came to questioning suspects. Roric didn't exactly play good cop, but Taven did bad cop better than anybody.

"Yeah, I think he's our best bet. These witnesses are useless." Taven followed him over to the cruiser and hopped in the front seat.

Derrick was chilling in the back, and Roric was surprised he wasn't putting up more of a fuss about being stuck there. He still didn't understand why Derrick had been so willing to implicate himself. Was he just a glory-seeking idiot, or was he trying to distract them from the real perp? Roric didn't think he was that smart, so he was leaning towards the first explanation even though Derrick didn't seem quite that dumb, either.

Roric had some handcuffs in the cruiser, so he cuffed Derrick before hauling him into the Agency. The new secretary, Veena, jolted when Roric shoved Derrick through the door. The older woman was alone in the office and focused intently on a television newscast about the breaking story.

Of course, she didn't look old. She'd retained her youthful appearance like all born vampires. But while his previous secretary, Serena, had dressed like the sexy twenty-something she was, Veena dressed more like a middle-aged mother in long, loose, floral dresses and practical flats. Serena was nice eye-candy, but Roric didn't miss her constant flirting.

He'd fired Serena when he found out she was associating with rogues. He suspected she might've been the mole who ashed one of their prisoners and gave the rogues insider information, but he had no proof. She'd disappeared after he fired her, though, presumably with her rogue boyfriend, and no one had heard from her since.

Roric could still hardly believe it, but yet it didn't surprise him. He'd taken her on one date before he realized that Serena had self-esteem issues and sought approval from anyone who would give her attention. She especially liked guys in authority. He hoped she'd come to her senses eventually and find someone better for her, and he really hoped he'd never have to arrest her. He cared about her even if he wasn't interested in her romantically.

"Agent Asheron, I'm so glad you're okay!" Veena jumped up and rushed over to him, her hands flapping like she wanted to hug him.

If he was honest with himself, he appreciated the way she mothered him since his own mother wasn't around to do it. She did the same thing to Taven, too. Taven complained about it, but Roric had a feeling his brother kind of liked it, too.

"What about Caroline and Ivy, are they alright?" Her face pinched with worry like they were her daughters.

"Yes, they're both fine, thank God."

Derrick snorted at that and made a face. Roric scowled at him and shoved him down the hallway.

"We're going to interrogate this suspect. Would you mind making us some coffee?" It wasn't that late, but he was mentally exhausted already.

"Oh, of course. I'll put on a fresh pot right now."

43

Veena scurried off into the briefing room where the coffeepot was at, her dress billowing behind her.

Roric pushed Derrick into the interrogation room and locked him into the thick, metal shackles attached to the table. He checked his pockets, pulling out a cellphone, some keys, and a wallet, and tossed them all aside. It wasn't exactly standard booking procedure, but he didn't care. Then he grabbed the clipboard with the interrogation form off the hook on the wall, sat down, and started filling out the basic information.

Roric had interrogated him before, and the dude hadn't responded to Roric's intimidation tactics, but Raven attempts to sympathize with him had managed to get him riled up enough to talk. Roric decided to go for a softer approach and let Taven be the bad cop, if necessary. Taven crossed his arms and leaned against the wall, glaring at Derrick, playing his part without Roric needing to say anything. Taven didn't know how to be anything but the bad cop.

"Okay, Derrick. You said you entered the school tonight, correct?" Derrick's earlier confession was useful, but having it on camera was better, and the cameras were rolling any time they were in the interrogation room.

Derrick leaned back in his chair as best he could with his arms shackled. "Nah, I didn't go in the school."

Roric frowned. "But you said you had a delivery to make."

"Yeah, but I didn't have to go in the school for that." He got a cocky grin on his face that Roric immediately wanted to smack off of him. He wasn't in the mood for games.

"What kind of delivery were you making?"

Derrick suddenly leaned forward and hissed at Roric. "A message."

Roric jerked but tried to cover it up by adjusting his grip on the clipboard. "A message? For who?"

"For you." Derrick's mouth curled in an evil smile.

Roric's heart started thumping. He clutched the clipboard tighter, his pulse pounding in his fingers, leaving damp fingerprints on the paper. "I'm listening."

"The rogues want you to back off. No school, no more Agency. It's time for you to accept that vampires are taking over. We won't be bound by laws created by humans, and we won't be policed by our own kind. We want the Agency shut down."

Derrick's voice was dead serious, but Roric couldn't help but laugh at him. "Are you crazy? We're not going to shut down the Agency. We're going to beef it up after this stunt."

"We've shown you what we're capable of. There are more of us than you can handle. You'll never be able to win. This is your one and only chance to surrender voluntarily. Shut down the Agency, and you can walk away."

"And if I don't, what? The rogues will come after me?" Roric wasn't laughing anymore. He should've known that the rogues would go after him eventually. It was just a matter of time.

"After they dispose of your family." Derrick's face curled up in that nasty grin again, and ice water flooded Roric's veins.

He suddenly remembered the way Derrick had watched Caroline and Ivy as they got in the car then started texting someone. Had this all been a set up to get to

Caroline and Ivy?

Roric jumped up, knocking his chair over, his heart attacking his ribcage like a wild animal trying to escape. He let the clipboard clatter to the table. He wasn't capable of speech, but he looked at Taven who was staring at him with the same look of dread etched across his face.

Roric quickly unlocked Derrick from the table and grabbed him by the arm in an iron grip. Taven yanked the door open, and Roric shoved Derrick through the door, down the hall, and into a cell. He slammed the door shut with an ominous clang that echoed in his chest. He needed to go find Caroline.

CHAPTER SIX

Caroline trudged towards Taven's cruiser, exhausted but wishing there was something, anything she could do to help. Maybe she should stay to comfort those who'd lost someone.

She turned back to look at the crowd. There were people crying, but none of them seemed to be alone. How much comfort would they get from a stranger? She didn't know any of them.

The only vampire she really knew was Roric, and he wanted her to go home. He'd been calm and respectful, asking her politely instead of demanding she obey him, and his face and voice were laced with anxiety. He wasn't just being overprotective or bossy, he really did have reason to worry. She should do what he asked if only to relieve some of his stress. He had a hard enough task to deal with without worrying about her. Maybe going home like he asked was the best thing she could do to help.

She let Ivy drive since she had the keys and they were taking Taven's car. Caroline climbed in the passenger seat and immediately turned down the blaring radio when Ivy started the car. The cruiser reeked of Taven's overpowering cologne, but it was comforting in a way.

Taven was like the brother she never had. She wasn't attracted to him at all, and she found his personality just as overbearing as his cologne sometimes, but he cared about her and treated her like a member of the family.

She felt the same way about Ivy. They were totally different, but dating brothers made them feel almost like sisters. Caroline appreciated having another girl around even if they didn't always see eye to eye. She hoped Taven and Ivy eventually mated. It would be awkward if they ever broke up, because she'd want to stay in touch with Ivy.

In typical sister fashion, as soon as they were alone in the car, Ivy started in with the girl talk. "Congrats on the whole mating thing. So, do you think Roric will get you a ring? Like an engagement ring? To be honest, I'm surprised he hasn't already."

Caroline chuckled and held up her left hand, examining her bare fingers. Everything about her relationship with Roric had been so unusual, she didn't know what to expect. "Do vampires give each other engagement rings like humans do?" She had no idea. She didn't even know any mated vampires personally.

"Beats me, but you should ask for one. Roric can afford it." Caroline saw Ivy take a glance at her own bare ring finger and wrinkle her nose.

She put a hand on Ivy's arm and looked over at her. "Taven will come around eventually. He loves you. You just need to give him time."

"I don't know. Did you hear him tonight? He doesn't have a very good opinion about mating. He wants to keep

48

his freedom." Ivy's face twisted in a snarl, and she clutched the steering wheel till her knuckles popped out.

"You don't actually think he wants to see other people, do you? I mean, he asked you to move in with him."

Ivy shook her head but didn't make eye contact. "I don't know. When we're together, he seems happy, but then he says stuff like that. I feel like he thinks he's going to get tired of me eventually, so he doesn't want to make a commitment."

From what Caroline knew about Taven, Ivy's suspicion sounded entirely plausible. But, of course, she didn't want to admit that to her friend. She wanted to warn her not to pressure him, though. That would probably make him run the other way. "So give him time to see that he wants you around for good."

"Maybe I should give him a chance to see that he can't live without me."

Caroline winced. She wasn't sure what Ivy had in mind, but it didn't sound like a healthy way to test the relationship.

They pulled up to the mansion then, and Ivy punched in the gate code and pulled around to the back of the house. She stopped by the back door but kept the engine running.

"I think I'm gonna go out, have a few drinks. No sense wasting this dress and makeup, right?" Ivy waved her hand over her still-clean outfit.

Caroline gawked at her. "What? You want to go to the bar after what happened?"

Ivy shrugged. "I mean, it was terrible, but it's not like I knew any of those people. The only person I'm close to is Taven, and he's busy. Why shouldn't I have some fun?"

Caroline face wrinkled in a frown. Did Ivy intend to

go out and find some other guy to be with? Something was going on in Ivy's head, and Caroline wasn't sure what, but it had her worried.

She knew Ivy didn't have any other friends or family. Was she feeling alone in the world after the way Taven acted? Caroline knew how that felt. She'd been alone for the last several years, till she met Roric. Maybe she needed to help Ivy see that there were other people who cared about her, people who needed her. They weren't exactly friends, but maybe Ivy needed one. Caroline could do that.

"I really don't want to be alone right now. I could use the company."

Ivy gave her a confused look. "You want to go to the bar with me?"

"No, I meant we could hang out here." Ivy was a lot more likely to do something regrettable if she was drunk at a bar.

"And do what?" Ivy still looked flummoxed. Obviously, she wasn't used to hanging out with girlfriends.

"I don't know. We could watch a movie, or something. Pop some popcorn." That was typical girls' night stuff, wasn't it? Caroline didn't really know, either. She hadn't hung out with a girlfriend just for fun since her parents died.

Ivy looked from Caroline to the house to her outfit.

"Please, Ivy. I need you."

Ivy sighed and turned off the engine. "Okay, I suppose I can stay in. But we're drinking wine, not soda."

Caroline smiled and opened the door. "Deal."

They headed inside. Caroline removed her heels, but Ivy tromped up the stairs in hers, the tall stilettos making a loud racket. The noise echoed in the stairwell, emphasizing how empty the house was. Roric, Taven, and their father were all out, and the housekeeper, Imelda, had the night off, so Caroline and Ivy were all alone.

Caroline was glad she'd asked Ivy to stay. The big, rambling mansion felt cold and foreboding, all of a sudden. She jumped when she heard a noise, but then she laughed at herself. It was only the old house settling. Her nerves were just on edge because of the bomb.

Caroline paused when they got to the top of the landing. "Where do you want to watch the movie?"

"Taven's TV is a lot bigger."

Caroline chuckled. "Of course it is. Does he have any movies?"

Ivy scrunched her nose. "Just a bunch of guy movies. Nothing good. What about Roric?"

"He's got a lot. I want to take off this dress, anyway. Why don't you come check out the movies while I change?"

Ivy nodded and followed Caroline to Roric's room. Caroline pushed open the door and pointed to the entertainment center under the TV. "All the movies are in there."

Ivy moved towards the TV while Caroline headed for the closet, dropping her clutch on the dresser. She stared at the closet door for a moment, surprised to see that it was closed. Roric usually didn't bother to close it. Since he kept it so neat and organized, he didn't mind having the contents on display. But they'd been in a hurry to leave. Maybe he'd made a mess in there and closed the door to hide it till he could clean it up. Caroline shrugged and opened the door.

There was no mess, but Caroline didn't think too much

about it. She unzipped her dress and let it fall to the floor. It was a dusty mess from the bomb. Hopefully the dry cleaner could get it back in shape. It was such a nice dress, it'd be a shame to only get to wear it once.

She slipped on some soft, black leggings and one of Roric's tee shirts, wanting to feel like he was with her. She'd agreed to mate with him tonight, and they weren't even going to see each other for hours, probably. After what had happened, she knew it was selfish and petty of her to be upset about it, but she couldn't help it.

After she was changed, she headed back into the room. Ivy was on her knees, still perusing Roric's movies. "Can't decide? If there's nothing that looks good, we could find something on Netflix."

"No, he's actually got a lot of good stuff here. Why am I not surprised that Roric likes chick flicks? Or are these yours?" Ivy held up a handful of romantic comedies.

Caroline chuckled. "No, they're his. I haven't seen most of them. I didn't spend much money on movies when I was single. Pick whichever one you like. I'm gonna go wash up a bit."

She turned and headed towards the bathroom but stopped when she got to the closed door — another one they usually kept open. Had Imelda been working tonight, after all? Maybe she'd come in here to clean while they were gone. That would explain it.

Caroline pushed through the door and closed it behind her then glanced in the mirror at her ragged appearance. Her hair was a wild mess, dust covered every inch of her body, and her tears had left streaks through the gray ash on her cheeks. Ash that was made up of the disintegrated bodies of dozens of vampires who'd lost their lives.

She might not have known them, but she grieved for them, all the same. In the past, she might have been happy to hear that there were less vampires in the world to worry about, but now she knew them as people not all that different from herself. She couldn't believe the rogues had killed their own kind like that, all in the name of freedom. She wished there was more she could do to help solve the problem, but this one was beyond her capabilities.

She blew her nose to clear out the dust then turned on the water with a sigh and grabbed her washcloth to clean the ashy remains off her face. With her nose clear, she realized the room smelled a little different than normal. Roric's cologne lingered in the air, but there was another scent, too. Not the cleaning products that Imelda used. This smelled more like another vampire. One she didn't recognize by scent. Had someone been in there?

She was just about to wash her face when the shower curtain whipped open and a vampire jumped out and grabbed her, wrapping one hand around her mouth and shoving a gun into her side. Caroline gasped, her mouth sucking at his damp palm, and she immediately tensed and grabbed for his arms, trying to remember the defense moves she and Roric had practiced. But he hadn't taught her what to do if there was a gun pointed at her.

"Don't move, don't make a sound, or I'll fill you full of silver, and my partner will kill your friend," the vampire hissed in her ear. Despite the sound of her heart pounding in her ears, the rushing water, and his barely audible whisper, his words were perfectly clear. Her body started to tremble.

"We're here for you, not her, so if you play nicely, we'll leave her alone. Do you understand?"

Caroline nodded and let her shaking hands fall to her sides. She didn't know if he was telling the truth, or not, but she didn't want to risk putting Ivy in jeopardy. And besides, he'd pump her full of silver if she tried to fight him.

She should've let Ivy go to the bar, then she wouldn't be in danger. Hell, Caroline should've gone with her! Why hadn't she noticed the strange scents when she walked in the house? Why hadn't she been more suspicious about the closed doors? She berated herself for all her mistakes. All she could do now was cooperate and try to keep from angering him.

"Good. Now, when I let go of your mouth, I want you to open the door and tell her that you're going to be a few minutes and you want her to go on to Taven's room. You got it?"

Caroline nodded again. The man let go of her mouth but kept the gun pressed into her side. He turned off the water, and Caroline stumbled over to the door and cracked it open.

Ivy looked up at her and held up a DVD. "How about this one?"

Caroline forced a smile, sure that her terror had to be obvious. "That looks great. While don't you go put it in, and I'll get us some popcorn."

"Don't forget the wine." Ivy grinned and walked out of the room, oblivious. Caroline flinched with each tap of her heels.

"Very good. Now we're gonna go downstairs. Keep your mouth shut and nobody gets hurt." The man pushed her out of the bathroom.

Caroline padded towards the door, eyeing her purse

with her phone in it, but there was no way for her to get it without the man noticing. She couldn't call Roric; she was on her own.

She stopped and peeked out into the hallway. No one was in sight, so she moved towards the stairwell. Was there really another vampire there? So far she hadn't seen anyone else. Maybe it was just a lie to keep her compliant.

Her mind spun with escape plans. When she got to Taven's door, she was just about to take a risk and turn on her kidnapper, hoping Ivy would hear her and come out to help her, when the TV turned on in Taven's room and another vampire stepped out of the room beside his.

There was no way she could take on both of them, and Ivy had less training in self defense than Caroline did. If she tried to help, they'd probably kill her like they threatened. Caroline's face twisted as she kept moving past the door. How was she going to get out of this?

They tiptoed down the stairwell, making only the tiniest squeaks on the wooden stairs. Caroline was barefoot, but there was nothing to do about it now. All her shoes were back in Roric's room.

As soon as they shoved her out the back door, she sucked in a giant breath of cool air. She felt like she'd been holding her breath for hours. She didn't see any vehicles other than Taven's cruiser. Were they leaving on foot? Caroline's hopes lifted some. That would leave a scent trail that Roric could follow. She was sweating so badly, her scent should linger for hours.

She wanted to run, but there was no place nearby to hide, and she knew the vampire wouldn't hesitate to shoot her. The gun had silver bullets, no doubt. They wouldn't kill her, but she'd be writhing in pain, helpless, until her body pushed them out. No, she couldn't afford to take the risk. She needed to wait for a better opportunity.

They led her down the driveway to the gate. It opened automatically when a car approached it from that side, but they didn't go near the sensor. Instead, the second vampire jumped up onto the tall, brick wall that surrounded the property then dropped onto the ground on the other side. That must've been how they entered the property. As a human, the wall surrounding the mansion had looked impressive to Caroline, but it was nothing for a vampire to scale it, even with thick bushes on either side of it.

The vampire with the gun waved it towards the wall. "Up and over, princess."

Caroline jumped up onto the wall for lack of a better plan. Her bare feet curled into the rough brick for balance. She hesitated there for a moment, hoping one of the neighbors would look out the window and see her standing there. But the humans who lived on this block were in bed by now, and the vampires were at the grand opening. There was no one around to help her.

The second vampire was down below, waiting for her. She dropped down next to him, and the other vampire followed right behind her. An old sedan waited for them half a block away.

The vampire with the gun climbed into the back seat, and the other vampire pushed her into the passenger seat. The vampire in the back pressed the gun to her neck while the other one got in and started the vehicle. They took off, into the night, their scents contained in the closed vehicle.

CHAPTER SEVEN

Roric and Taven raced out of the Agency without bothering to explain themselves to Veena and jumped into Roric's cruiser. Roric peeled out of the parking lot, barely bothering to check for traffic. Thankfully there wasn't much at that time of night. He switched on his lights and siren, anyway, and blasted down the road going double the speed limit.

Steering with one hand, he dug his phone out of his pocket and commanded it to call Caroline. It rang and rang, but there was no answer.

Roric jabbed at the phone to end the call when her voicemail came on. He didn't think he could handle speaking, but he managed to tell Taven to try Ivy. Her phone rang several times before it went to voicemail, too.

"Ivy, call me. Now," Taven barked into the phone then hung up and looked at Roric.

"Their phones are probably still on silent. They probably just can't hear them."

It was a plausible explanation, and Roric nodded in agreement, but deep down he knew it wasn't true. He could feel it in his bones.   Something was very wrong. Only mated vampires were supposed to be able to sense each other like that, but Roric could feel the threat to her like someone had a gun to his head.

He slammed on his brakes at the drive leading to the family mansion, wishing he could ram through the gate instead of waiting for it to open.   He jabbed the code into the keypad and pounded his fists on the steering wheel as the gate slowly swung open.   As soon as it was wide enough for the car to get through, he jammed his foot on the accelerator and squealed up to the house.   He pulled around back and felt a touch of relief at the sight of Taven's cruiser.

But as soon as they jumped out of the car, his nose caught a whiff of Caroline, Ivy, and two other vampire scents he didn't recognize.   Caroline's scent was pungent with fear. A cold chill shivered through Roric's body.

He breathed in deeply, following the scent down the driveway.   Taven followed behind him.   The scent veered off to the side before it got to the gate and wafted over the bushes. Had they jumped the wall?

He leapt to the top.   Sure enough, Caroline's scent lingered there.   He dropped to the other side and smelled her again, but the scent trail only went a short ways before it disappeared completely.   Roric's whole body turned to ice like his blood had frozen solid.

Had they gotten in a car and driven off? If she had, he had no chance of tracing her.   He couldn't accept that, not until he'd eliminated every other possibility.   He forced his body to move, shattering the ice that engulfed him.

"I don't smell Ivy.   Only back by the car," Taven said when Roric leapt back over the wall onto the driveway.

"Let's check inside." Roric dashed to the back door at vampire speed, and Taven followed him.

He yanked the door open, yelling for Caroline and Ivy, but no one responded. Their scent trailed up the stairs, along with the unfamiliar scents. Roric followed it, his body working on autopilot. His brain was still frozen.

The door to Taven's room was open, so Roric stepped inside. Ivy's scent was fresh in the space, but there was no trace of Caroline's or the other vampires'.

A DVD was queued up on the big screen TV, the menu playing a couple bars of a peppy love song over and over again as pictures of a happy couple flashed across the screen. Roric wanted to throw something at the TV to shut it up so he could hear, but there was no point. When his eyes scanned the space, he quickly realized there was no one in there.

Taven scoped out the bathroom and closet, even though they were obviously empty, while Roric headed back into the hall. He followed Caroline's scent down to his own room. That door was open, too, and Caroline's scent was strong there. But so was one of the other scents. Terror coiled in his belly like a snake, preparing to bite him. He was moving carefully, trying to charm it, but he knew it would strike any moment.

There was no sign of a struggle, no blood anywhere. He felt the tiniest bit of relief at that. Caroline's scent went into the closet where her dress lay on the floor then led to the bathroom. The scents were stronger there. He could smell her fear and one of the other vampire's nervousness.

He moved back into the living space and noticed Caroline's purse lying on the dresser. He dug into it and pulled out her phone. A missed call from him flashed on the screen when he pressed the home button.

Taven stood at the door, glancing into the room. "Ivy's scent goes this way." He pointed towards the stairs at the opposite end of the hall that led down to the kitchen.

Roric nodded and followed him. Roric's heart seized when he got halfway down the stairs and heard noises coming from the kitchen. He leapt the rest of the way down, landing at the bottom with a thunderous crash.

He whipped around the corner to see Ivy, dressed in plaid lounge pants and a black tee shirt, opening cupboards. She jerked around at his crash landing and gawked at him. "Roric?"

Taven was behind him on the stairwell. He shoved Roric out of the way at the sound of Ivy's voice and rushed over to her, lifting her up in his arms till her feet dangled between his knees. Ivy gasped but smiled at him and wrapped her arms around his neck.

"Oh, thank God, you're okay." Taven let Ivy slide down his body till her feet were on the ground again, but he didn't let go of her. Instead, he lowered his lips to hers and kissed her till Roric thought he was going to explode.

"Where's Caroline?" he barked out, grabbing Ivy's shoulder and tearing her away from Taven.

"I don't know. I was waiting for her to bring the popcorn, but she never showed up. I thought maybe she couldn't find any in your suite and came down here to look for some. What's going on?" She glanced nervously back and forth from him to Taven.

"The witness we arrested said some things. We thought you might be in danger." Taven stroked her hair and shoulder, looking relieved.

But Roric's nightmare was just beginning. Taven

could never complain about taking second place to Roric ever again. Not after this. Because of their positions, Taven's woman was safe in his arms, while Caroline was God-knows-where, her life in danger.

"I think they took Caroline." Roric admitted the truth he'd known ever since he smelled those strange vampires. Ever since Derrick mentioned his family.

He didn't know what else to do, so he searched the whole house top to bottom, looking under beds and inside cabinets like she was a child playing hide-n-seek. But Caroline's scent was nowhere that he hadn't already been. She was gone, and he had no idea how to find her.

When he'd made a complete circuit around the entire mansion, he collapsed on the cold, hard floor in the kitchen, wishing it could numb his burning, aching heart. Guilt pounded on his body like an attacker beating him with a baseball bat.

Why had he sent her home without him? He knew the rogues were on the offense; he never should've let her out of his sight. And why didn't he have better security in place, here and at the school? Was he so overly-confident that he thought nothing could ever touch him? The rogues had been ramping up their attacks for weeks; he should've anticipated something like this!

He'd been teaching Caroline self defense, but obviously that wasn't enough. He tried to picture the kidnapping. Had she fought back? There was no sign of a struggle, but that didn't mean she'd gone easily. What if they'd knocked her out? Was she injured and in pain right now, terrified and counting on Roric to save her? His body shuddered in sympathetic spasms of anxiety.

Taven kneeled down beside him and put a hand on his

shoulder. "We'll find her, bro. They're not going to kill her; they want her as a bargaining chip. They'll make contact and say something that we can use to track her down. Then we'll bring her back, safe and sound, and beat these rogues at their own game."

That wasn't a plan, that was an idle threat made by someone who had no hand to play. He couldn't just sit around and wait for someone to give him a clue. He had to *do* something.

He jumped up off the floor. "I'm going back to the Agency to interrogate Derrick. He knows something, and he's going to talk if I have to squeeze it out of him with a silver straight jacket."

Roric didn't wait for Taven to respond. He just rushed out of the house and jumped in his cruiser. A few minutes later, he was back at the Agency. He glanced down at his filthy suit, knowing his face and hair had to look just as dirty. He probably should've taken a shower while he was at home, but he didn't want to waste a minute. Caroline was waiting for him, and he couldn't let her down.

He didn't even bother to take Derrick to the interrogation room, he just thundered into the cell block, wrapped his hands around the bars of Derrick's cell, and shook them like he was trying to knock them down. "Where is she? Where'd they take her? Tell me if you ever want to get out of here."

Derrick jumped up off his cot and sauntered over to Roric with a smug look on his face that Roric wanted to bitch slap off of him. "I don't know anything, and I didn't do anything. You don't have any evidence that I planted that bomb. I demand to be released."

Roric's lips peeled back in a snarl. "I can keep you

here for 24 hours, and I can do whatever I need to do to restrain you. Start talking, and I won't pump your body full of silver and accidentally leave your window blinds open."

Derrick sneered and called out to the other prisoners in the adjacent cells. "Did you hear that? He's threatening to kill me."

Roric pulled out his gun and aimed it just past Derrick's head then pulled the trigger. The silver bullet slammed into the concrete wall with an ear-shattering bang that echoed up and down the cell block. The burning scent of gunfire burst out in a cloud. Derrick screeched and jumped around, his eyes bouncing around the cell as the bullet ricocheted, but it didn't hit him. Roric didn't care if it did. He kept the gun pointed at Derrick.

"At this point, I'll kill any rogue who gets in my way, and after tonight, the public will commend me for it. Now tell me what you know."

Derrick's eyes were wide and wild, and sweat beaded up on his forehead. He backed as far away from Roric as he could, his body shaking. "I told you, I don't know anything, man. I was just supposed to distract you for a while and give you the message. That's all I know."

Roric shook the bars again, his face hot and tightened into a menacing scowl. "Who told you to do that?"

Derrick stuck his hands up in the air. "Just a guy. I don't know his name, I swear."

Roric sneered at him. "So you were willing to do what this total stranger wanted for no reason other than he asked you to? Willing to get yourself thrown in jail? Willing to risk being charged with planting a bomb? Are you really that big of an idiot?"

"I had to, alright? My creator told me to." He looked off into the corner as he spoke.

Roric nodded slowly, understanding dawning. "So even rogues follow some authority. Who's your creator?"

Derrick's eyes bugged out again. "I can't tell you that, man! If she finds out, I'll be dead."

Roric pointed the gun at his face, trying not to let his surprise show at the use of the feminine pronoun. "If you don't tell me, I'll kill you before she has a chance to. Now spill."

Derrick rubbed a hand over his buzzcut hair. "Fine! Her name's Layla Wilson, but she's not the one behind this. The guy in charge is Michael. I've never met him. I don't know his last name or what he looks like."

Roric didn't recognize the name, but that was no surprise. It was probably a lie. "Where do I find Layla?"

Derrick shook his head. "I don't know where she lives."

Roric fired another round at Derrick's feet. "Don't mess with me, Derrick! I don't have time for this. Now tell me how to find Layla!"

Derrick jumped and stumbled backwards then fell onto his ass. "I swear, I don't know! I've never been to her place."

"What does she look like?"

Derrick stared off like he was picturing the woman. "Tall, thin, shoulder-length dark hair, gray eyes, 30-ish."

That was pretty specific, probably the truth. Roric ran through his memories but couldn't think of anyone he knew who fit the description, but there were way more rogues out there than he wanted to admit.

"How'd you meet her?"

KELLIE MCALLEN

"At a bar. The Speakeasy."

"Does she go there a lot?"

Derrick shrugged. "I don't know. We don't hang out."

"But you see her sometimes. She told you to do what Michael wanted."

"Yeah, sometimes." Derrick shrugged again, and Roric wanted to put a bullet through his shoulders.

"Where do you see her? When do you see her? I want answers, damn it! If you won't give them to me, I have no use for you." He slammed a hand against the cell, rattling the bars on the door, and gave Derrick a look that hopefully emphasized how willing and eager he was to kill him.

Derrick's face contorted, and he squirmed backwards till his back hit the wall. "I bring her people, and she lets me drink from her."

"What kind of people?"

"People who might be willing to be turned and join our ranks."

Roric's face twisted in disgust. So they were actively recruiting. It was another piece of evidence that the rogues were more organized than he dared to admit.

"So, you call her when you get somebody and she meets you somewhere?"

Derrick sighed and put his head in his hands. "Yeah."

Roric nodded. "Now we're getting somewhere. It's time for you to make a phone call."

CHAPTER EIGHT

Caroline gasped as the vampire in the seat behind her pulled a black fabric sack over her head and cinched the drawstring tight around her neck, knotting it in back. The world went black, and her lungs tightened. Her breath sped up, short quick, erratic breaths, but there wasn't enough air. Her fingers immediately dug into the small gap between the bag and her skin.

The vampire thumped the gun against her skull, rattling her brain. "Leave it! You're not suffocating. If you won't cooperate, I'll have to put you out."

Caroline sucked in a deep breath and held it, her whole body trembling. She knew what that meant. Either a stake to the heart, or a bullet to the head. She'd seen firsthand how a vampire turned to stone when they were staked. They were completely vulnerable and as good as dead unless someone pulled the stake out. She remembered her shock when she'd seen Roric's body staked and lifeless and the horror she felt when she did the same to Houston.

She'd never seen a vampire with a bullet in the brain, but she'd heard about the gruesome injury. The bullet had the power to enter a vampire's thick skull on its own but not enough to exit. It would bounce around inside the skull, causing terrible pain and scrambling the brain till the vampire was braindead. The vampire's body would work to expel the bullet from the skull, but the vampire would be a vegetable until it healed. It took a long time, and the vampire wasn't always the same when they came back. Caroline couldn't imagine anything worse for her kind to endure.

She dropped her hands in her lap and wrung her fingers as her eyes squeezed tight against her hot tears. They dripped down her cheeks anyway, but she didn't dare reach up to wipe at them. Would he really do that to her? She didn't know, but she didn't want to risk it.

They drove for a long time, making several turns. Caroline tried to figure out where she was, but she lost track after a while. She had a feeling they were driving aimlessly, trying to confuse her. Eventually, they pulled to a stop. The vampire behind her kept the gun to her head, so she sat still and waited for the driver to come around and open her door.

He took her arm and pulled her out of the car then led her up a short flight of stairs and into a house or building, she wasn't sure which. Her nose tickled with the pungent, musty scent of mold and rotting wood under several layers of vampire. She wanted to rub at it, but she kept her hands out in front of her to keep from running into anything. Her captives allowed her that, at least.

They led her around a corner, through a narrow hallway, and down a set of creaking, wooden stairs that bowed in the middle. Eventually, they pushed her into a room and stopped. One of them worked at the knot in the drawstring then loosened the bag and pulled it over her head. She squinted against the bright light coming from a fixture in the ceiling. When her eyes adjusted, she could see the two men who had invaded her home. One of them held the gun out, pointed at her.

"Behave, and you might get to go home again. That is if that boyfriend of yours cooperates." He gave a cruel leer then backed out of the room. The other man followed him. They yanked the door shut with a solemn thud then turned two deadbolts on the other side. The locks clanked into place with a cold finality.

Caroline glanced around the room, quickly assessing her prison. Four gray, cinderblock walls, cool and almost damp, and a concrete floor. No windows. Since she'd walked down a set of stairs, she assumed she was in a basement. A strong, well-fed vampire could bust through concrete with enough effort, but if she was underground, it wouldn't do her any good.

The ceiling looked like drywall. Maybe she could jump up and break through it, but there'd be a wooden floor above that. She'd make so much noise trying to get through it, they'd surely hear her.

The only door was the one she came in. It was metal, so she couldn't break through it. She might be able to kick it down, despite the two deadbolts, but it would make a ton of noise, and she didn't know if anyone was on the other side.

Her fear ratcheted up another level, her body shivering with anxiety. Was it cold in there, or was it just her fear? She was desperate to escape, but there was nothing she could do. She had to be patient and cooperate until she gathered more information. If she attempted to escape and failed, they'd make her pay for it, and then they'd ramp up the security.

She probably wouldn't even be there that long. Roric would figure out what happened as soon as he came home. Actually, Ivy would call him as soon as she realized Caroline was missing. He was probably already looking for her.

Her face crumpled, imagining how he must be feeling. He was always so concerned about her. Imagining his pain was worse than her own anxiety. If he thought she was in danger, he'd go crazy. Hopefully he could keep a level head so he could find her.

She had no idea how he'd track her down, though. Her scent trail ended when she got in the car, and she didn't think the security camera at the gate could see the car from where it was parked. But her kidnappers hadn't killed her which meant they wanted to use her to get something from Roric. They'd be in contact with him.

Caroline slumped down on the mattress lying on the floor in the corner, covered with dingy sheets and a thin, pilled blanket. She trembled as the endorphins dissipated, and her clenched muscles tried to relax. They ached from the tension. Her whole body felt heavy with exhaustion.

She put her face in her hands and let the tears fall. They dripped out slowly at first, but eventually they poured down her cheeks, soaking her hands as her body was wracked with sobs. She was strong, independent. She'd faced the worst possible traumas and come out stronger. But today was too much.

The bombing, searching through the remains for Taven and Ivy, the kidnapping, even agreeing to mate with Roric — it was an emotional overload. She could take whatever life threw at her, but not all at once. Maybe she could save herself from this, but she didn't want to. She wanted Roric to rescue her. She needed him to hold her and tell her that he would take care of her.

Maybe that made her weak, but she didn't care. She was tired of doing everything on her own. She was going to mate with Roric. That meant they were partners, and she could rely on him to help her. She had to trust that he would.

She laid there for what felt like hours but could've been only minutes, staring at the gray walls, trying to make her mind as blank, but no matter how hard she tried, her brain whirled with anxious thoughts. She trusted Roric, she did, but she had no idea how he'd ever find her. Maybe he'd have to give them whatever they wanted. But what did they want?

Eventually, the locks on the door clicked, and the door swung open. Caroline was too lost in her own mind to notice until the door closed again. A man she didn't recognize stood in front of it, staring down at her with blue eyes as clear and bright as the summer sky that contrasted with his dark-as-night hair. His face was handsome, but he had a look of malice that his sculpted features couldn't hide. He wore his deceptively simple black pants and button down shirt with ease, like they were custom made to fit his body.

"Caroline, I can see why Roric likes you. You're even prettier in person. Although, I have to admit you're a bit of a mess."

Caroline cringed when he leaned down and stroked her hair then took a deep sniff. "Who are you?"

He shook his head, his lips quirked in a wry smile.

"It's ironic that you're nothing, but yet I know you so well, and I'm the most influential vampire in this city, but you have no idea who I am."

Caroline's face froze as a chill went down her body. Was he the leader of the rogues? What did he know about her? She'd been with Roric for a few months now, but she stayed out of the spotlight. Tonight was the first time Roric had taken her to a public function and introduced her. Had this man been spying on them?

"You're surprised by this. A man in a position of power must know his opponents well if he wishes to stay there. I believe your leader has failed to fully educate himself about his enemy. Everything we do seems to catch him by surprise."

Caroline's first instinct was to lash back with a dozen insults, but she forced them all down. This man held too much power over her to risk angering. She had to be docile and pretend like she would cooperate, even as her mind constantly searched for ways to escape. Maybe she could learn something useful if she kept him talking.

"What's your name?"

"My name is Michael. I'm the leader of the rogues, but I like my privacy. Very few people get the opportunity to meet me. But like I said, I like to know my enemies, and you seem to be very important to Roric Asheron." He stared at her like he was trying to unearth her secrets. His eyes blazed like a blue flame, his stare burning away all the lies.

"You were turned, not born. Quite an unusual choice for him, a born vampire with a strong allegiance to his kind. Roric never dated a turned vampire before you. What was it about you that captured his interest?"

KELLIE MCALLEN

Caroline breathed out a ragged sigh of relief. It didn't sound like he knew the truth, even if he suspected something. "Roric is a compassionate man. He likes to help those in need, and I needed his help. We fell in love."

Michael put his hands in his pockets and leaned against the wall. "Yes, I can see he's very committed to you. How fitting that he announced your engagement at tonight's event. Of course, he had no idea what I was planning. How foolish of him to be so unprepared. I'm eager to see how deep his commitment goes. How far is he willing to go for you?"

"What do you want from him?" Caroline hated the fearful quiver in her voice.

"I want him to bring an end to this ridiculous attempt to regulate vampirism. He's nothing but a pawn for the human government. Once the Agency concedes, the vampires can unite as the true rulers of this world." He threw his arms out like a preacher in the throes of a passionate sermon.

Her eyes bulged, and her body quaked. She wrapped her arms around her knees. "You're going to ask him to shut down the Agency?"

Roric's world revolved around the Agency. He believed in the law, believed it was the only way that vampires and humans could live in peace with each other. But this man didn't want peace, he wanted the vampires to take over.

Roric loved her enough to break the rules for her once, but she couldn't expect him to give up everything he stood for just to save her. She couldn't ask that of him, even if he was willing. She had to find a way to save herself before this man put Roric's allegiance to the test.

Michael gave her a benign smile that couldn't mask his evil intent. "No, you're going to ask him to."

CHAPTER NINE

The staccato beep of an incoming text woke Piper from a deep sleep. Who the heck was texting her in the middle of the night? She slapped a hand towards her nightstand, searching for her phone in case it was something important. She managed to pry her eyes open just enough to make out the words on the screen.

I'm okay

It was from her brother, Alec. What did that mean? Why wouldn't he be okay? Piper pulled herself into a semi-upright position and squinted at the screen as she typed back a question mark.

There was a bomb at the school

Piper's eyes popped open. She jerked upright and put a hand to her chest where her heart was currently trying to kick its way out.

The grand opening event at the Academy! It was supposed to be a big shindig. She would've liked to have gone, but since she wasn't a high-ranking vampire, she didn't get an invitation.

She wasn't a vampire at all, at least not yet, thanks to

her annoying brother. He could've invited her to go with him, but no, he didn't want her anywhere near vampires, even though he was one. Traitor.

Of course, those thoughts immediately brought Davede to mind. He would've been at the party, probably. Was he okay? Her mind was suddenly jumpy with worry. She pulled up his contact then typed out a quick text. It was only after she hit send that she wondered how he would take it.

She hadn't seen much of Davede lately, not since that night he'd offered to change her. She wanted it more than anything, but she wasn't sure she could accept his one condition. He didn't want her to be with anyone but him. What he really wanted was for her to mate with him, but there was no way she was ready for that.

She liked Davede. He was cute, and nice, and she enjoyed his company, but he wasn't exactly the typical vampire. He wasn't wild, or intense, or dangerous, or any of the things that made her so interested in them.

Of course, none of that mattered to her brother. Davede was probably the nicest vampire out there, but Alec had a conniption when he found out Piper was dating him. He'd threatened to fire Davede if he didn't stay away from her.

Alec didn't want Piper volunteering at the blood clinic, either, but she'd put her foot down about that. She was 22 years old, a grown woman with a career and everything. He had no right to tell her what she could and couldn't do, even if he was in charge of the blood clinic. They desperately needed human volunteers, and she was addicted to the erotic rush of having a vampire feed off her.

Alec had finally conceded, figuring that it was better

than her dating a vampire, but he didn't know that she was looking for one who'd be willing to change her, no strings attached. She thought Houston might have done it if she'd asked, but he got thrown if jail before she worked up the nerve.

Davede didn't seem quite as eager to change her once Houston was out of the picture, and she'd passed on his offer, knowing he wanted more of a commitment than she was willing to make. But thinking about him being in danger made her suddenly realize how much she cared about him and missed him.

Her phone beeped again, this time with a text from Davede. *I'm okay. Thanks for asking. I'm surprised you're awake.*

She breathed out a sigh of relief and tapped on his avatar, enlarging the picture. His handsome face smiled back at her. She hated the thought of him being hurt, or worse, dead.

My brother just told me what happened. I was worried about you, she typed back.

I miss you

His words hung in the air between them like he was right in front of her, staring at her, waiting for her response. She wished he was there for real so she could see him, touch him.

I miss you, too. She typed it out and hit send before she had a chance to think about what she was doing. She never was any good at keeping her thoughts to herself. Whatever she was feeling fell right out of her mouth.

Could I see you again sometime? He immediately asked.

She knew that was coming. Was that what she

wanted? Davede wasn't a casual dater. He was looking for something serious. She shouldn't toy with him if she wasn't interested enough to pursue a relationship with him. But she really wanted to see him, all of a sudden. She couldn't stop herself from replying.

I'm free tomorrow

Davede responded with a smiling cat emoji. An emoji! What kind of vampire used emojis? But she chuckled all the same.

Pick you up at 7?

She texted him back that 7 was fine then sent him a purple heart emoji. Red was too intense, pink was too sweet, but purple was enigmatic, just like her feelings. Plus it was her favorite color, as evidenced by her bedroom decor. She slumped back down on the bed and pulled her comforter over her head.

What was she doing? Was she going to start dating Davede again? To what end? Was she reconsidering his offer? All it would take was one promise, and he'd give her what she desperately wanted. But could she give him what he wanted in return?

She should've gone back to sleep, but she was too wired to keep her eyes closed. Instead, she turned on the TV and flipped through the stations till she found a news report about the bomb. The images and body count were horrifying. She always thought of vampires as invincible, but dozens had been killed. Were any of them her friends?

She clutched her comforter to her chest as she watched the footage, rumpling the purple satin. She sighed when she caught a glimpse of Roric. If he was questioning witnesses, that had to mean that he and Caroline were okay. She'd call her tomorrow, after things settled down.

Piper had wanted to be a vampire ever since her brother was turned, maybe even before that, but now she had second thoughts. She knew she'd never be able to become a vampire legally. Her brother would never allow her application to be approved. With all the recent attacks, she thought it would be easy to pretend she'd been attacked and turned by a rogue. But maybe that wasn't such a good idea now. After this, the Agency was sure to crack down on newly-turned vampires. She figured if she was turned she might have to spend a few months in the school, but if the school was destroyed, they might do something more drastic, instead.

She wanted to be a vampire, but the world didn't look at them the same way it used to. In the beginning, after the shock wore off, the vampires portrayed themselves as peaceful, civilized creatures, and humans had started to accept them. But now, vampires were becoming the enemy. If they kept creating chaos, the humans were going to go on the offensive.

Was she willing to risk destroying her reputation? She might lose her job. She didn't love being a middle-school art teacher, but it was a living. She tended to jump into things without thinking them through, but maybe she needed to show a little restraint this time. But if that was her plan, why was she going out with Davede tomorrow?

She wrestled with her conflicting desires until she finally fell asleep again. When she woke up, her thoughts weren't any clearer, but she knew she had to see Davede. Just to assure herself that he was okay. At least, that's what she told herself.

She fussed over her clothes for half an hour, unsure what to wear since she didn't know what they were doing, in either sense of the word. What vibe did she want to give off? She had no idea.

She eventually settled on nice jeans and a pretty, green blouse that matched her eyes and complimented her red hair. The outfit looked feminine but not too sexy. She kept her daytime hair and makeup and spritzed on just one squirt of her favorite perfume. Of course, vampires tended to prefer the natural scent of human blood to any fancy fragrance.

When Davede rang her doorbell a couple minutes before 7, she rushed to answer it but then forced herself to calm down and take a deep breath. She knew she had a dopey grin on her face, but she didn't care. She couldn't wait to see him.

He seemed to appreciate her smile, if his own was any proof. It lit up his face, making him look more handsome than she remembered. His chocolate eyes got all gooey at the sight of her. He pulled his hands out of the pockets of his dark jeans and reached towards her but then stopped halfway between them like he wasn't sure it was okay.

She grabbed him around the waist and pressed her cheek up against his chest. His aqua dress shirt felt stiff against her skin, but his muscles were firm and smooth underneath. At least he'd left it untucked and rolled up the sleeves so it looked casual. She wrapped her hands around his back and slid them up to stroke his broad shoulders. She liked how big he was. Despite the fact that he was a total softie inside, his vampire body was all thick, hard muscle.

He stroked her, too, and she wondered if he liked her soft curves. She was small, but she didn't work out, so she didn't have much muscle definition. The way he touched her made her think he liked her just fine the way she was, though.   Sparks tingled everywhere his long fingers caressed.

She wanted to keep touching him, but it was going on long enough he might get the wrong idea, whatever that was, so eventually she pulled away enough to look up at him. "I'm glad you're safe. Was it horrible? It looked horrible."

She took his hand and led him into her apartment then plopped down on the couch. The bright turquoise sofa seemed too garish for such a serious conversation, even if it suited her personality. Davede sat down next to her, close enough that their thighs were touching. He propped an elbow up on the back of the couch and turned towards her, leaning his head on his hand, his face suddenly somber.

"It was the worst thing I've ever lived through. The whole night, I kept wishing I had asked you to go with me, but then I was so glad I didn't." He lifted his head and let his hand drop down to stroke her cheek.

"You wanted me to go with you?" Her hand rubbed nervously at the velvet nap of the sofa.

"Of course. I'm still interested in you, Piper. You're the one who's not sure about this." He waved a hand between them then let it fall to his lap.

"But what about your job, and Alec, and... stuff?" She wanted to take his hand, but instead she twisted her fingers together in her lap.

He shook his head. "Alec can't fire me for dating his sister, although I'm sure he'd be happy to turn me in to the Agency if he knew I'd drunk from you. I'm hoping he won't ever find out about that."

His eyes darkened like bitter dark chocolate. "I don't

like that you're feeding other vampires at the clinic, but I have no claim on you, so I have no right to be jealous. I admit I'm glad that Houston guy isn't around anymore."

She dropped her eyes to her lap, too ashamed to meet his gaze. "I'm sorry about that. I told myself it was okay since we hadn't defined our relationship, but I knew it would hurt you if you found out. I shouldn't have done that. Can you forgive me?"

She dared to peek up at him, and his eyes were like warm cocoa. "I'm here, aren't I?"

"I'm glad." She couldn't resist any longer. She leaned in and placed her lips gently on his. He reached out and grabbed her around the waist, pulling her closer, and her body melted against his. He caressed her mouth with long, slow kisses, like he was savoring the taste of her. She wondered if he wanted to drink from her, but for the moment he seemed content just to kiss her.

Eventually, he pulled away, breathing hard. Her whole body hummed with desire, and Davede looked like he felt the same way. They'd never had sex, never gone farther than a few, soft kisses. Not because she didn't want to but because Davede was a gentleman who seemed content to take it slow. Was he ready to take it up a notch?

"Piper? I want you, and I'll do whatever it takes to have you." His eyes glimmered with intensity, and his mouth was slightly open, revealing the tips of his descended fangs. His hot breaths puffed against her face.

She wanted it so bad, but for once in her life she knew she needed to resist her urge to jump in headfirst. "Why don't we try dating again for a little while first? And maybe a few more of those kisses? Clothing optional."

Davede's lips curled in a smile, and he pulled her

forehead to his. His eyes dropped down to the vee of her blouse that draped open enough for him to see her cleavage from that angle. "I really like this outfit you're wearing, but I wouldn't mind seeing what's under it."

CHAPTER TEN

Roric retrieved Derrick's cell phone from the interrogation room and tried to check it out, but he couldn't get past the lock screen. It didn't matter; if Derrick wanted to live, he'd do whatever Roric asked him to. Roric was in no mood to be challenged, and he'd proven that to Derrick already.

He held up the phone and waved it at Derrick once he got back to his cell. "What's the password?"

Derrick stiffened like he wanted to resist, the tattoos on his biceps stretching as he clutched the cell bars, but Roric put one hand on the gun at his side and raised an eyebrow. Derrick was smart enough to give him the right code. Roric scrolled through his contact list, looking for what, he didn't know, but he felt like there was too much he didn't know about the rogues. He'd thought they were just that — rogue vampires who didn't want to play by the rules, but an attack like tonight's took a lot of planning and a level of organization he never realized they had.

On one hand, it scared him to think what they were capable of and what they might be planning, but on the other hand, if he could get to the head of their organization, he might be able to bring down the whole operation. He'd find Caroline then find their leader and take him out. The rogues would scatter like cockroaches, and he and his agents would stomp them out.

He found a contact named Layla and held the screen up for Derrick to see. "Is this your creator?"

Derrick nodded.

"Alright, listen closely. I'm going to dial the number and hold the phone, and you're going to talk. You're going to tell her you did your job and you have somebody to bring to her. Arrange a meeting for as soon as you can. If you say one thing out of line, I'll put a bullet in your brain. I'm past the point of playing by the rules, as you can probably tell. If this goes off without a hitch, I'll let you go. We clear?"

Roric made no promises about the future, in fact, he fully intended to ash Derrick as soon as he lost his usefulness, but he needed to take full advantage of him first. Derrick gulped and nodded.

Roric was just about to tap on the number when one of the other rogues started banging on his cell. That wouldn't do. He didn't want Layla to know that Derrick was still in jail. He shoved the phone back in his pocket and opened Derrick's cell then dragged him to the interrogation room. He shackled him to the table and pulled out the phone.

It rang twice, then a gravelly, female voice said, "Did you do your job?"

Derrick got twitchy, and his voice raised an octave. This woman obviously had his balls in a vise. "Yeah, yeah, of course. No problem."

"How did he respond?"

Derrick glanced nervously at Roric before answering.

"He got mad and took off to look for Caroline."

"He didn't ask how to contact us?"

There was no easy way for Roric to tell him what to say, so he had to trust that Derrick would come up with something good. Derrick wasn't an idiot; he could figure it out. Roric pulled his gun out and stroked it as a reminder of why he should.

Derrick gulped, his eyes flicking from the gun to Roric's face. "Naw, he was too worked up. But he knows where I live. He'll come around when he's ready to cooperate."

The woman's voice got softer, sexier. "Very good. I'll have to reward you."

Roric nodded, pleased with Derrick's response, and rolled his hand, indicating that Derrick should keep going.

"I've got somebody for you. When can we meet?"

The woman chuckled — deep, throaty, the kind of laugh that made most men's dick hard. If she looked anything like she sounded, Roric could see why Derrick was willing to do whatever she asked. "So ambitious. So eager to please. Are you at home? I wouldn't mind celebrating tonight's win with you."

Roric nodded again. The sooner they met, the sooner he could find Caroline. He didn't want her to suffer a minute longer.

"Uh, yeah, I'm on my way there. 20 minutes?" He flicked his eyes towards Roric.

"Make it 30. That will give you time for a shower," the woman said.

Roric wanted to laugh at the dig — Derrick was a little scuzzy — but he was too on edge. He held his hand out for the phone as soon as Derrick disconnected the call.

"Good job. Your brain stays bullet-free for now. Let's go to your place, and you can introduce me to your friend, Layla. If all goes well, you can go back to your pathetic life soon."

Roric unshackled Derrick from the table but cuffed his hands behind his back. He'd been able to handle him on his own so far, but he'd feel more confident if he had a little help. Maybe he should call Taven. The bastard was probably in bed with Ivy, celebrating the fact that they were both alive and well and together, while Roric was scrambling to save his town and his woman.

Roric was cussing out his brother in his mind when he yanked open the interrogation room door and just about ran into him. "I thought you were busy with Ivy."

"You need me more than she does right now. Get any more info out of him?" Taven glanced at Derrick.

Roric's scowl softened a bit. "Yeah, we're going to his place to meet his creator, see if we can get some info out of her about their leader."

Taven gawked at him, just as surprised as Roric had been. "You can explain on the way."

Then he turned and headed back towards to front of the office. Roric stopped by his secretary's desk on the way out, figuring he ought to let somebody know where they were going in case things went to hell.

A few minutes later, they neared the small, old house where Roric had first apprehended Derrick a few months ago. Roric didn't see any cars there yet or any other vehicles lurking nearby, so he pulled up to the house and held out Derrick's keys to Taven. "Take him inside. I'm going to park the cruiser somewhere out of sight."

Taven nodded and jumped out then hauled Derrick out

of the back seat and up the front walk. Roric pulled around the corner and parked his cruiser in the driveway of a house with tall bushes blocking out most of the view from the street. Then he footed it back to Derrick's house.

Inside, the place looked exactly how Roric would've imagined it — plain, white walls dirty with fingerprints around the light switches and doorways, worn out, mismatched furniture, beer cans, take out boxes, and dirty cups and plates littering the living room. It stank of rotten food and stale beer. He took a quick peek around the house to get a handle on the layout then Taven did the same.

Roric unlocked Derrick's cuffs when Taven came back into the living room. Derrick perched on the arm of the sofa and rubbed his wrists, and Taven kept an eye on the street, peeking through a slit in the blinds. Roric didn't want to touch anything, so he paced back and forth across the stained, matted carpet instead as he explained the plan to Derrick.

"Okay, when Layla gets here, you're going to open the door and let her in. When she asks about your recruit, I'll come out of the bedroom. Taven will be hiding nearby, keeping an eye on you. If you try anything, you'll be braindead before you have a chance to regret it. You got it?"

Derrick nodded and rubbed a hand over his buzzed hair, his body twitchy and reeking of nervous sweat. Roric thought about making him take that shower so he could stand to be around him, but he didn't want to make him any more comfortable than necessary. Roric was almost as anxious, but he savored the rush of adrenaline coursing through his veins like gasoline. It gave him the energy he needed to push through the fear that would otherwise cripple him.

He didn't need to tell Taven what to do. Taven instinctively knew how to deal with a perp and work a scene like this. If he was honest, Taven was probably a better field agent that he was, but Roric was more mature and levelheaded, with a better brain for strategizing and a dedication to upholding the law, qualities that made him a good leader. Although, he felt like he was always two steps behind the rogues lately.

When a car pulled up, Taven stepped away from the window and squatted behind a chair, out of sight but close enough to pounce if Derrick tried anything stupid. "Show time."

Roric nodded and moved down the hall towards the bedroom. It was a little cleaner than the living room, but not much. The rumpled sheets on the bed were grimy and yellowed with stains Roric didn't want to guess at. Clothes lay in piles on the floor. Half-empty cups and wadded tissues crowded the nightstand.

Roric stood still and held his breath when he heard Derrick open the door to Layla then let the air out slowly when Derrick shut the door. He'd passed the first test by not immediately running when he had the chance.

"You didn't shower," was the first thing Layla said when she walked in the house, and Roric stifled a laugh, but then he heard sounds like they were kissing. Apparently Layla didn't mind too much. He wished he could see what was going on, but he could imagine it. He wondered what this woman looked like. She must be pretty if she got Derrick all hot and bothered, but what decent-looking woman would be interested in him? He was a total sleaze bag, in Roric's opinion.

"So, where's this new recruit?" she said when the kissing sounds stopped.

Roric took that as his cue and headed back towards the living room. The woman jerked when she saw him come around the corner.

"You must be Layla. I'm Roric." He stuck out a hand to her, and she gawked at him like he was a crazy person. He kept his hand out, though, and eventually she reached out a tentative hand and shook it.

She had a decent figure, medium-length dark hair, and unique gray eyes like Derrick had described, but her face didn't live up to the rest of her. Her beak nose was too prominent, her lips too thin, and her eyes were too close-set for her to be considered pretty.

As soon as Roric let go of her, he clamped a hand around Derrick's bicep and pulled his gun out. Layla eyed it nervously. "Derrick gave me your message, but he was foolish enough to let me bring him in to the station. We had a little talk, and he realized the error of his ways. But unfortunately, it seems like Derrick doesn't know anything useful. But he agreed to introduce me to you, and in return, I agreed not to pump him full of silver and leave his body by an open window."

Layla turned to Derrick and hissed at him. "You fool! I told you to distract him, not get yourself arrested!"

"I'm sorry, babe! His brother jumped me as soon as I said I had a delivery to make." Derrick jerked towards Layla, but Roric held him back.

"Now, I assume you're not high enough up in the chain tot know where Caroline is. Or am I wrong?" Roric goaded her, hoping she'd say something useful, trying to prove her status.

She gritted her teeth and snarled at him but didn't respond, so he tried another tactic. "Derrick has informed me that there's a man named Michael who orchestrated this whole event. I want you to tell me how to find him."

Layla's eyes bugged out as she whipped her head towards Derrick. That was enough for Roric to know that was the truth. "Why would I tell you that?"

"Because if you don't, I'm going to kill your friend here in front of you."

Layla gulped but then tossed her hair and stuck her chin out. "I don't care about him. He's nothing to me."

Derrick flinched like she'd slapped him. Roric wasn't completely surprised, though. He pointed the gun at Derrick's head and pulled the trigger. The blast boomed through the small house, shaking it, and Derrick dropped to the ground, blood pouring from the hole in his head. Taven leapt out behind Layla.

Roric scowled at her, putting all his rage into one fierce look, and swung the gun her way. "Caroline is my mate-to-be, and I'll kill anybody who stands between us. Now, tell me how to find Michael."

She threw her hands up in the air and jerked when she backed into the butt of Taven's gun, storm clouds building in her gray eyes. "I don't know, all I have is a number."

"Then call him. Tell him I want to talk to him." He nodded at Taven who reached into her back pocket and pulled out her cell phone.

She gave up the password, and Taven quickly located the number. He hit the call button then put the phone on speaker and held it close to her. It rang a few times, then a male voice came on.

"This is Layla. I need to talk to Michael."

While she waited, Roric pressed the gun to her temple. The butt of it was still warm from the last shot. "Layla, I'm gonna give you one more chance. Tell me where I can find Michael if you want to walk out of here. Otherwise, I have no more use for you."

"I swear, I don't know. Please don't kill me." She shook her head, her body visibly trembling. He believed her. He lowered the gun but kept it aimed at her middle.

Another man's voice came on the line, this one more polished, sophisticated. "This is Michael."

Taven held the phone up to Roric. "This is Roric Asheron. I believe you have something of mine."

The man had the audacity to let out a musical laugh. Roric's fist squeezed the gun, and he wanted to shoot a few rounds just to release some of his anger.

"I have something of yours, too. Layla and Derrick. Actually, I have at least four more of your pawns in lockup. I'll trade you."

"Half a dozen to one, that's quite a bargain. Only I think we both know that Caroline is worth a lot more to you than those lackeys are to me. Do what you want with them. They're easy enough to replace. I assume they've already told you my terms. Make a public announcement declaring the permanent closure of the Agency and lock the doors. We'll take care of the building for you." He laughed again, like it was nothing but an amusing game for him.

Roric's body shook, the gun wobbling in his hand, and he could feel his face heating up, the skin pulled tight by his rage as he bared his fangs. "I won't give in that easily. The Agency is the only thing keeping vamps like you from destroying everything."

"Hmm, I thought Caroline meant more to you than

your job, but maybe I was wrong. Oh well, it was worth a shot. I'll give you two days to make up your mind. If I don't hear from you, I'll dispose of your little mate-to-be, and we'll have to do this the hard way. We're prepared for battle. Are you?"

Roric howled and reached for the phone, ready to hurl it across the room, but Taven anticipated his move and yanked it out of his reach, disconnecting the call. "We might need that number again."

Roric shoved the gun to Layla's temple again and pulled the trigger, needing to release his anger somehow. She crumpled to the ground with a heavy thud, her eyes clouded and her mouth open. Her blood joined the pool soaking into the filthy carpet.

CHAPTER ELEVEN

Caroline stared intently at the garish, orange, 5-gallon bucket in the corner, the only item in the room besides the mattress, but no matter how hard she tried, she couldn't think of a way to use it to facilitate her escape, other than tossing her own reeking waste at her captors. Even if she could somehow disable them with the lightweight plastic, she still needed an opportunity, and it didn't seem like she was going to get one anytime soon. No one had been in to check on her in hours.

They obviously felt no reason to. Vampires could live for weeks without food, water, or blood, so they didn't need to bring her anything. Going without would diminish her strength, but that would only work in her captors' favor. They knew as well as she did that there was no way for her to escape her prison.

The only hope she had was that Michael would come back to have her call Roric. Maybe if he did she could attack him and run away. It was a ridiculous plan. She had no idea who or what was on the other side of the door, but she doubted she'd have a clear path to freedom. Even if she managed to overpower Michael and escape the room, there were most likely rogues on the other side of the door who would thwart her. It would be foolish to even attempt it. But the only other option was to wait for rescue. She had no idea if it would ever come, or not.

She hated the feeling of being out of control, waiting for someone else to decide her fate. Anxiety made it impossible for her to rest, even though she was dead tired, and depression seeped into her bones, sapping her of any strength she had left. If an opportunity ever did present itself, she'd be too exhausted to take advantage of it.

That was proven to her later when the locks clicked and the door swung open, but Caroline barely moved her head to see who was entering. But she jerked upright, making herself dizzy, when she recognized the long, brown hair and bright pink lips on a familiar face. Serena. Roric's former secretary who'd disappeared after Roric fired her when he found out she was associating with rogues.

"Serena?" She'd replaced her sexy business wear with tight black jeans and a slinky, black top, obviously trying to fit in better with the rogues, but she looked more urban chic than intimidating.

"Hello, Caroline." She had a plate of food and a bottle of water in her hands, and she held them out to Caroline.

Caroline gave her a bewildered look but took them. The peanut butter sandwich and apple looked and smelled more appealing than any food she'd ever eaten. The ache in her empty belly had gotten lost amidst her other worries, but now that she had food in front of her, it roared to the forefront of her complaints.

The peanut butter clung to the roof of her desiccated

mouth, gluing her tongue and making it hard to swallow, but it was sweet and filling, the protein, carbs, and sugar instantly satisfying. It was only after she'd taken several bites of the sandwich that she realized it might not be safe to eat it. But she didn't immediately pass out or feel her stomach burning with poison, so apparently it wasn't contaminated.

She quickly scarfed down the rest of it, alternating bites of the sandwich with chunks of fresh, juicy apple, while Serena watched her. Afterwards, she guzzled the entire bottle of water and wished she had another. Or a blood bag.

Once her hunger was sated, her mind was able to focus on the person who'd delivered the life-giving sustenance that made her feel a hundred times better. She knew Serena was dating a rogue, and Roric thought she might have been leaking information that gave the rogues an advantage over the Agency, but she never expected her to be in their inner circle.

"Serena, what are you doing here?"

Serena tossed her hair behind her shoulder with an irritated eye flick. "I knew they weren't feeding you, and I felt bad for you."

Caroline flushed and nodded. "Thank you, but I meant what are you doing with the rogues?"

"I'm dating Leon. He's one of the guys who brought you here — the cute blond one. He's Michael's right hand man." She smiled like she expected Caroline to congratulate her on bagging such a great boyfriend.

"Serena, you worked for the Agency. You've always been a model vampire. How can you associate with these... people?" There were a lot worse words she wanted to use to describe them, but she didn't want to offend Serena. Having her here was an unexpected boon. Not just because she'd been kind enough to bring Caroline food, but because she knew her. She had to feel some sympathy for her.

"He's not a bad guy, Caroline. He just wants the freedom to live his life on his own terms."

In other words, without any laws to prevent him from doing whatever he wanted, no matter who it hurt. He'd kidnapped Caroline and presumably participated in the bombing that had killed dozens of innocent vampires, plus, since he was a rogue, he most likely drank from humans against their will and changed others into vampires. Caroline didn't understand how Serena could see him as anything other than a bad guy, but she gritted her teeth to keep from blurting out her rebuttal.

"Is that what you want, too? Is that why you're with them?"

Serena shrugged and pulled on the hem of her shirt. "I don't really care about drinking from humans, but I don't think we should have to do what humans tell us to."

Caroline knew that all Serena really cared about was having the approval of someone important. She'd been interested in both Roric and Taven in the past, but they'd rebuffed her. She must've decided that she had a better chance with the other side. Caroline was positive they had taken advantage of her to get insider information, but it wouldn't help her case any to point that out to Serena.

She decided to try appealing to her sympathetic side, instead. "Serena, I'm not an agent. I don't make the rules, and I don't enforce them. I don't deserve to be treated like this. Will you please help me?"

Serena gestured at the empty plate and bottle. "I am helping you. That's why I brought you food. They don't want to hurt you, they just want to get Roric to shut down the Agency."

"He can't do that. Not even for me." Her voice held all the pain of that truth.

Serena waved her arms around. "The Agency is going down eventually. The rebellion is getting bigger and stronger every day. Roric has to see that."

"You know him, Serena. You know he won't give up that easily. He won't go down without a fight. How many more vampires have to die?" Caroline clenched at the edge of the grimy mattress, her body overcome with pain at the thought of any more death.

Serena crossed her arms and leaned against the wall. "That's up to Roric. If he gives up now, it'll be over. All the vampires will be free to do what they want, and the rogues will leave the other vampires alone."

Caroline shook her head. She wasn't getting anywhere trying to persuade Serena to help her escape. But maybe she could manipulate her some other way.

"I'm going to be here a long time if they're waiting for Roric to give in. I'm so filthy. I'm covered in vampire ash from the bomb. Can you at least let me go to the bathroom and wash up?"

Serena wrinkled her nose and glanced from Caroline to the bucket in the corner. "It does stink in here. Let me see what I can do. I'll be back."

She took the plate and bottle from Caroline and turned her back on her to unlock the door. Caroline was tempted to attack her from behind, but she was sure there were other vampires around. She had to scope out the place first before she tried escaping. She'd only get one shot. She had to make it count.

Serena came back a few minutes later with her boyfriend who had the gun in his hands. Caroline's hopes plummeted. He'd shoot her down the moment she tried anything.

"Okay, Leon said I could take you to the bathroom," Serena said.

"But one wrong move, and I'll put a bullet in your head." Leon waved the gun at her, scowling.

Caroline nodded and stood up, trying to look sufficiently intimidated. It wasn't hard since she was. "I understand. I'll cooperate, just please don't hurt me."

Serena wrapped a hand around her arm and led her out of the room while Leon walked behind them, pressing the gun into her back.

Outside the room was a large space with the same cinderblock walls and concrete floor. Three metal poles divided the space, supporting the floor above them. A few dusty boxes piled in one corner and a set of bare, wooden stairs were the only other things in the space, no other signs of occupancy. Caroline's hopes lifted a little when she realized they didn't have anyone guarding the room where she was held. They probably didn't think there was any way she could escape it.

Serena guided her up the stairs and through a wooden door at the top that opened into a hallway. They walked down it then turned a corner into a foyer area. On one side was a wide, dark-stained wooden door with a small, arched decorative window in the top that let in a ray of sunshine. It shined a crescent of golden light on the hardwood floors like a mocking smile — her natural enemy, the sun, promising freedom from her captors if she stepped into its jaws.

She turned her head the other way and saw a living room, furnished with masculine, black leather sofas and heavy, wrought iron tables with thick, glossy wood tops. A couple vampires sat in the room, drinking and talking. They looked up and eyed Caroline but didn't say anything, probably because Leon was right behind her with a gun.

Serena turned the brass knob on a nearby door that opened into a tiny bathroom. With a tub on one wall and a toilet and sink on the other, it wasn't big enough for the both of them. Serena let go of Caroline's arm, and Caroline walked in, staring at the small window on the back wall.

Leon snarled and waved the gun at her. "We'll be right on the other side of this door. You try anything, and we'll hear it."

Caroline nodded, knowing it was the truth, and shut the door. With that many vampires around, there was no way she could escape, even though the outside was just a few feet away from her, taunting her.

She pulled open the gold and navy shower curtain that reminded her of the color scheme in Roric's suite, pierced with a pang of longing. Would she ever go back there, or would her life end in this house full of her enemies? She wanted the comfort of a warm shower and the time to think, so she turned on the water and stripped off her clothes.

She sighed as the hot water hit her tense, knotted muscles and rinsed away the grime coating her skin. Ash pooled on the bottom of the tub and ran down the drain. Her tears followed it. She grieved for all the vampires whose lives had disintegrated in the fatal blast and whose bodies had been scattered into a million dust fragments that would be washed down the drain like they were nothing but dirt.

Caroline mourned for a long moment until the tub rinsed clean, then she forced herself to move on. There was nothing she could do for the dead, but she still had a life she might be able to save if she could come up with a plan. There was nothing in the shower except for a bar of soap and bottles of shampoo and conditioner. She peeked around the curtain at the bathroom again, looking for anything useful.

The towel bar was flimsy metal that looked like it would bend before it did any damage. The top of the toilet tank was heavy porcelain; she could probably use it to knock down a vampire temporarily. But there were too many others nearby; they'd surround her and take her down.

She leaned over and opened the cabinet door under the sink, but there was nothing there except for a few rolls of toilet paper and some cleaning products. What would happen if a vampire got sprayed in the eye with a chemical? She didn't know, but she doubted it would slow them down for long.

The medicine cabinet held a tube of toothpaste, some toothbrushes, a comb, a wrapped bar of soap, and a few other things she wanted to use, but nothing that would help her escape.

She glanced at the window again. Could she open it and jump out without them hearing? She pulled the blinds back to look more closely. The old, metal locks were rusty with age, and the wooden sash had several thick layers of paint on it. It would probably make a loud screech if she tried to push the window open.

But the window was surrounded by wooden trim. If she could pry a piece of it loose, it would make a perfect stake. She could hide it in her clothing and use it when she got a good opportunity. The curtains would cover up the missing wood; no one would notice it was gone. But how could she detach it from the wall without them hearing?

She pulled her head back into the shower and grabbed the shampoo, thinking while she sudsed up her hair and rinsed it off. When the soapy bottle almost slipped from her hand, she had an epiphany.

Keeping the water running, she quietly stepped out of the shower and started exploring the window trim. She was able to pry up the edge nearest the shower a bit with her fingers. If she timed it right, she thought she could make another noise that would distract them from the sound of her yanking the wood loose.

Climbing back in the shower, she stuck one hand out of the curtain and lodged her fingers under the loose edge of window trim. She slid her other hand behind the bottles of shampoo and conditioner. She spread her legs, bracing her feet against the sides of the bathtub.

Taking a deep breath, she simultaneously knocked the bottles to the bottom of the tub and yanked the wood loose. The heavy bottles tumbled down with a loud clatter, and a long, jagged chunk of the wood snapped off easily in her strong hand.

"I just dropped the shampoo bottle," she hollered out, yanking the hand with the wood back behind the curtain at the same moment that the bathroom door flung open.

She quickly stuck the stake between her thighs, pressing her legs together to cover it. Serena pulled open the shower curtain and looked at her. Caroline gasped and crossed one arm over her breasts and tried to cover her crotch with the other hand, holding her breath. Hopefully, Serena would think her racing heart was due to embarrassment. Serena glanced from her to the bottles laying on the bottom of the tub then pulled the curtain shut.

"Sorry, Leon made me check." She exited from the bathroom before Caroline had a chance to respond.

Caroline let out a long breath and pulled the stake out with shaking fingers, setting it on the edge of the window behind the curtain. She took a few more minutes to condition her hair so her breathing and heart rate could return to normal. When she finally felt calm again, she got out, dried off, and put her clothes back on.

She wished she had something cleaner to wear, but at least her body wasn't covered in vampire ash any longer. But she felt totally rejuvenated and full of energy. With her new weapon, she had a surge of confidence for the first time since Leon pressed the gun to her back in her own bathroom.

She quickly hid the stake in her leggings. Thankfully, her long tee shirt covered the bulge. Then, since no one was rushing her to get out, she used the comb she'd seen earlier to tease the tangles out of her hair and one of the toothbrushes and the paste to clean her teeth.

When she was done, she called out, "Coming out," and slowly opened the bathroom door.

Leon and Serena were waiting for her on the other side. They escorted her back down to her room in the basement. Caroline pressed her arm against the chunk of wood so they wouldn't notice it and tried to keep her heart rate and breathing steady.

Someone had emptied her bucket and rinsed it out, so all she could smell was the damp, moldy scent seeping through the walls and the lingering scent of her own body odor that had gotten trapped in the bedding. It made her want to gag after the fresh, clean scent of water, soap, and shampoo, but she didn't complain. She wanted Leon and Serena to get out of there so she could stash her weapon.

She turned to Serena and gave her the biggest smile she could manage. "Thanks, Serena. I really appreciate it."

"When Michael gives you a chance to talk to Roric, tell him to give in, Caroline. If he doesn't, Michael will kill you."

Caroline gulped and nodded. As soon as they left, she pulled the stake out of her leggings and shoved it under the mattress. She had a lot of planning to do, quickly.

CHAPTER TWELVE

A thoughtful boyfriend would've tiptoed into the room and slid quietly into the bed so he wouldn't wake up his sleeping girlfriend, but Taven had never been known for his sensitivity, and all he wanted was to wrap his body around Ivy and find some relief from his stress. He clomped into the room instead, his dress shoes leaving a trail of ash to the bed where he kicked them off. Then he pulled his shirt over his head, popping a few buttons, dropped his pants, and climbed into bed, reaching out for Ivy. And found nothing.

His hands scrambled around the satin sheets, and he eventually sat up and yanked the covers off — it was a big ass bed, after all — but nope, her side of the bed was empty. Where the hell was she?

"Ivy?" he barked out into the dark room. Silence.

He switched on the bedside lamp, casting a soft, yellow glow around the black and red room, but she wasn't in there. Grunting, he hauled his exhausted body out of the bed and shuffled over to the bathroom, pushing the door open. The room was dark, which should've been enough to tell him she wasn't in there, but he flipped on the lights, anyway, blinding himself. He squinted into the brightness reflecting off the glossy, white marble, but the bathroom was just as empty as the rest of his suite.

Fear filled his body like wet concrete, cutting off his air supply. His limbs were too heavy to lift, but he knew if he didn't keep moving, his body would be cemented in place, frozen with panic. He forced himself to turn around and start searching the house.

He felt guilty about it, but he'd been so relieved when he found out the kidnappers hadn't taken Ivy. For once in his life, he was glad he wasn't in his brother's position. He couldn't imagine what he'd do if someone had stolen his woman right from his own home.

He'd thought she was safe. The kidnappers had come and gone, taking Caroline but leaving Ivy. Taven had hugged and kissed her, reassured that she was safe, then he'd left to go help Roric search for Caroline. Had he made the biggest mistake of his life, leaving her alone here?

He tore through the house like a madman, calling her name. His voice sounded like a tortured kitten, mewling in desperation as he searched room after room but came up empty. By the time he'd circled back around to his suite, his chest was so tight, it ached with each ragged breath he dragged in through fiery lungs, and every heartbeat felt like a stab wound.

He grabbed his pants off the floor and dug through his pocket for his cell phone. No missed calls or texts. He pulled up Ivy's number and tried to control his heavy breathing as it rang. Straight to voicemail. His hand squeezed around the phone, wanting to crush it, but he managed to stop himself before he destroyed it.

The locator app! He jabbed his finger against the screen, and the app popped open — a map of the city with little blue dots representing the few people in this town he cared about. Roric, Caroline, and Ivy.

Caroline's dot hovered over their house since that's where her cell phone was. They still had no idea where she really was. Could be a million different places, maybe somewhere not even on the map of Modesa. Roric's dot showed him roaming the streets, searching for a clue to Caroline's whereabouts and probably agonizing about the deal Michael had offered him.

Taven didn't envy him one bit tonight. What would he do if he had to choose between the woman he loved and the cause he'd devoted his life to? Taven knew what he would choose, but he wasn't as committed to the cause as Roric was. Roric had a tendency to do the right thing no matter what, except when it came to Caroline. He'd broken every rule for her, but would he sacrifice the Agency for her? Taven didn't know, but he was sure as hell glad that he didn't have to make that decision.

Ivy's dot was just a few blocks away, at their favorite hangout. Had she gone to the bar? Taven grabbed his dirty clothes off the floor and pulled them on again then shoved his feet into his shoes. He probably should put on something else besides the monkey suit he wore to the grand opening, but he didn't care what he looked like. He pounded down the stairs, threw himself into his cruiser, and took off, burning rubber as he squealed out of his driveway and made the quick drive to Benders.

It was one of the few bars in town that stayed open most of the night, so the parking lot was full even though it was almost dawn. Taven didn't bother searching the lot for her car. Ivy's gorgeous body would be a lot easier to spot than her plain, black Civic.

He stomped inside, his eyes immediately scanning the crowded, smoke-filled space lit mostly with tacky beer signs. A few women leaned against the battered wood bar top, several more were shaking their ass on the dance floor to the pounding rock music, and others were sitting at the tables. But the only one he was interested in was standing too close to a dude in a cowboy hat and dusty boots, smiling and laughing, still wearing the sexy, red dress and heels she'd worn to the event.

Relief flooded his body at the same time anger welled up in it, the two conflicting emotions crashing into each other, knocking him off balance. He staggered over to her, stars flashing across his vision, and grabbed ahold of her.

She jerked her arm back at the sudden pressure and gawked at him. "Taven! What are you doing here?"

"What am I doing here? What are you doing here?" He whipped his head around at the crowd of people enjoying the night like they didn't have a care in the world while his world was being ripped apart. How could Ivy come here like it was any other night?

"You were gone. You left me alone, so I came here for some company."

He should've told her how worried he was, how he'd thought she'd been kidnapped, how he'd freaked out at the thought of losing her, but when she flicked her hair back like it was no big deal, his anger shoved his worry out of his focus.

"I was busy looking for Caroline!" he growled at her. He hadn't wanted to leave her, but obviously, his brother's kidnapped girlfriend took precedence.   Couldn't she understand that?

The cowboy glared at him then flicked his eyes towards Ivy. "Who is this guy?"

Taven scowled at him, baring a fang.   "I'm her boyfriend."

The cowboy held up his hands and backed up a few feet. "Whoa, I didn't know you had a boyfriend. I don't want to invade anybody else's territory."

"Then get lost." Taven hissed.

The cowboy disappeared into the crowd. Ivy rolled her eyes and leaned against a nearby chair. "Geez, Taven. We were just talking. What do you care, anyway?"

His face flamed red hot with rage. How could she think he didn't care? "What the hell, Ivy? You live with me! That doesn't mean anything to you?"

"We're not mated. You don't own me." She leveled her gaze at him, daring him to contradict her.

He raked a hand through his hair and started pacing back and forth in the small space that had cleared around them when they started fighting. "Of course we're not mated! How could I ever mate with you if I can't trust you not to run off to someone else the minute I'm away? God, Ivy! This is exactly why I never wanted another serious relationship."

Memories of his last serious girlfriend flashed through his mind. He'd loved Talia with all his heart, given her every part of himself. But when he'd asked her to mate with him, she turned him down and ended it. Later, he found out she'd started seeing someone else while they were dating. She mated the guy a few months later. Ever since then, Taven had been too afraid to give his heart to anyone else, but somehow, Ivy had managed to steal it.

Ivy moved closer and hissed at him through clenched teeth so no one else could hear. "Then why'd you turn me, Taven? Why'd you ask me to move in with you? If that's the way you feel, than why are we even dating?"

The words popped into his brain and came out of his mouth before his heart had a chance to weigh in on it. "I don't know, Ivy. Maybe we shouldn't be."

He should've told her how much he cared about her, how he didn't regret turning her for a minute, how he loved having her in his home and his bed, how he wanted her to be his forever, how he was terrified of losing her.

But his fear took over. He thought if he admitted those things to her, then he gave her the power to destroy him, but she already had it. Not telling her how he felt only motivated her to use it.

She leveled her gaze at him, her emotions hidden so deep inside her dark eyes he was afraid he'd fall in if he got too close. "I guess we're done, then."

He gawked at her, speechless. She stared at him for a long moment then turned away and walked off without looking back. Taven's legs gave out under him. He started to fall, but a chair caught him. He fumbled into it and dropped his head on the nearby table. The wood felt cool against the burning heat of his face. He closed his eyes and let the chaos around him engulf him. What had he done?

CHAPTER THIRTEEN

Caroline felt like the character in "The Princess and the Pea," only it was a wooden stake poking at her through one thin mattress. She knew she was only imagining it, but it felt like the wood dug deeper into her back the longer she laid there till it was imbedded in her spine. Maybe it was trying to give her the backbone she needed to make a move already.

She'd been waiting for the perfect opportunity, but it felt like hours had gone by without anyone coming in. Maybe she needed to make her own opportunity. She thought about banging on the door in hopes that someone would come check on her, but the timing was critical to her success, and she had no idea what time it was. There was no clock or window in the room, and her stress had distorted her sense of time till she couldn't tell the difference between hours and minutes.

How long had she been there? It felt like days, but she doubted they'd keep her that long. Surely there was a time limit on their offer. After that, they'd kill her and try something different. Serena had already said as much. If she waited for the perfect moment, she might run out of time before it ever arrived.

She had convinced herself to take action but was still working up her nerve when the door swung open, like her thoughts had conjured up a visitor. Caroline gasped and quickly stuck her hand behind her back, hiding the stake she'd been practicing brandishing.

Serena had a plate with another sandwich in one hand and a water bottle in the other. Caroline wasn't hungry; she was too nervous to think about food. But if Serena was bringing her another meal, it had probably been at least four or five hours since her last visit, maybe even more.

The sun had been out when she went upstairs, but most vampires slept during daylight. The fact that several vampires were awake then meant the sun had probably just risen or was about to set. But Caroline wasn't sure which. Was it still daylight? The information was crucial to her plan. She decided to see if she could get some answers out of Serena before she made her move.

She slid the stake under the blanket behind her then reached out to take the food and water. "Is it dinnertime already? I can't keep track of the time in here."

Serena handed it over. "It's after dawn. I'm heading to bed, but I thought you might be hungry."

"Thank you." Caroline tried not to react to the news, but inside, her body was flooded with endorphins. Sunrise meant most of the vampires would be tired and ready for bed if they weren't asleep already. There would be less chance of running into one once she got upstairs.

The only problem was, if she went outside, she'd burn up in the sun. Her legs were covered, and she could pull her arms inside her shirt, but her head and feet would be exposed. There were hats on a rack by the front door that she could steal, but what about her feet? She didn't have any socks or shoes. She quivered, imagining the pain of running while her feet were blistering in the sun. They'd only last a few moments. Her body's reaction gave her an idea.

She set the plate and water bottle down on the bed then rubbed her hands up and down her arms and massaged her bare feet. "It's so cold and damp down here. My feet are freezing. Do you think you could get me a pair of socks?"

Serena shrugged. "Sure. I guess so."

Caroline gave her a grateful smile. "Great, thanks."

As soon as Serena left the room, Caroline grabbed the stake and waited by the door. She held the stake out in front of her with both hands, ready to attack. Her heart beat a frantic rhythm, and her breath came in quick, ragged gasps as she waited for Serena to return. Her hands got so damp and shaky, she was afraid the stake would slip right through her fingers. She wiped them off one at a time on her pants then tightened her grip around the chunk of wood.

When she heard the locks turn again, she sucked in a deep breath and braced her feet shoulder-width apart, bending a little at the knees like Roric had taught her. As soon as Serena stepped through the door, Caroline lunged for her, impaling her. The stake pierced Serena's thin blouse and lodged in her chest, stopping her heart on impact. Serena dropped to the ground, frozen, the closest a vampire came to human death. She didn't even get a chance to scream.

Caroline almost did, though. But she muffled herself, slapping a hand over her mouth so only a tiny squeak came out. She quickly peeked out the door to see if anyone had witnessed the attack, but like earlier, the rest of the basement was empty. She dragged Serena into the room so she could shut the door. Then she grabbed the socks from Serena's hand and pulled them on.

Serena didn't have anything else useful, except the key to the door. Caroline extracted it from her fingers and stuck it in the waistband of her leggings. She hesitated for a long moment, looking at the stake, debating whether to take it or not. As soon as she removed it, Serena would come back to life. Caroline could lock her in the room, but Serena would no doubt make a racket that might alert the others.

But if she left the stake, she'd be weaponless. A stake wouldn't be much defense against a gun, and she could only use it to take down one vampire, but she had the element of surprise on her side. Without it, all she had was her fledgling knowledge of self-defense which hadn't been enough to prevent her from being kidnapped.

She glanced around the empty room that contained nothing but a mattress covered in sheets and a waste bucket. An idea dawned on her, and she rushed over to the bedding and tore three strips off the sheet. One of them she wadded up and shoved in Serena's mouth. The next she tied around her head, keeping the gag in place. The other one she used to tie her hands and feet together behind her back, looping the fabric around and around to strengthen the binding. Serena would break through it quickly, but hopefully it would give Caroline a few minutes.

Grinning at her ingenuity, she yanked the stake out of Serena's chest and rushed out the door, locking the deadbolts before Serena had a chance to recover from the staking. She could hear Serena struggling on the other side of the door, but it was quiet enough that hopefully no one upstairs could hear it.

Her heart was pounding so loudly, she couldn't hear anything else, so she forced herself to wait for a moment and take some long, slow breaths. When she'd calmed down a little, she scurried over to the stairs and tiptoed up them as fast as she could, staying to the sides so the steps would be less likely to creak under her weight.

Her heart started racing again when she got to the door at the top of the stairs, but there wasn't much she could do to calm it. The next few minutes were going to be intense, and her body knew it. Instead, she embraced the surge of energy. She was ready to run out of there, but she had to force herself to be as careful and quiet as possible.

She slowly twisted the knob and cracked the door open, peering out through the tiny space into the hallway. It was empty, so she opened the door and slipped out. She couldn't afford to linger in the hallway. It ran down the center of the house, and several doors opened up into it. Someone could step out of one of them at any moment and see her.

She padded down the hall till she got to the corner then stopped and carefully peeked around it, trying to keep from exposing herself. The living room had the most chance of being occupied, so she looked that way first. She sucked in a deep breath when she saw a vampire sitting there.

But his back was to her, and he was looking down at his lap like he was reading something. He didn't seem to notice her presence, although she was sure her body was sending out clouds of nervous pheromones. Maybe there were enough vampires that came and went that he didn't think anything of it.

She turned her head the other way, towards the front door. The foyer was empty, and the door to the bathroom was cracked open and the lights were off, so she doubted anyone was in there. All she had to do was take a few steps and open the door, then she'd be free.

She sucked in a deep breath to fortify herself then rushed towards the door as quickly and quietly as she could. With the hand holding the stake, she grabbed a hat off the nearby rack and shoved it on her head, and with the other she turned the locks and twisted the handle. The door swung open with a small creak, and daylight streamed around her, blinding her. She ducked her head, letting the brim of the hat shield her face from the deadly rays. Then she stepped out into the sunlight.

Suddenly, a dark shadow blocked out the sun. Hands grasped her arms, locking them at her sides. She looked up into the sinister face of Michael. His lips curled in a smile like he was happy to see her.

"My, my. Isn't this just perfect timing? A few moments later, and you might have actually escaped. I'm anxious to find out how you managed this, but first, let's get out of this dreadful sun."

He pushed her back inside, his hands digging into her arms like clamps. Caroline tried to resist, tried to make an offensive move, but he was stronger than her, and she couldn't stop the momentum that had her stumbling backwards into the house. He kicked the door shut behind him.

"Beckett!" Michael bellowed out, and the vampire in the living room came running. He yanked Caroline's hands behind her back and held them tight in his iron grip, taking the stake from her.

Michael let go of her arms and pulled a gun from his belt. He aimed it at her heart, pressing the cold, metal muzzle hard against her breastbone. "Let's go back downstairs, shall we?"

She knew it was futile, but she was so close to freedom, she had to reach for it. If she let them put her back in that room, she'd probably never get out. She slammed her head forward, butting Michael in the forehead. He staggered backwards, stunned, and the vampire holding her arms jerked in surprise.

She took the opportunity to wretch her arms free of his grip, then she jabbed her elbow backwards into his ribs with a loud grunt. When he bent and clutched his side, she whirled around and shoved her palm into his nose, crushing it. Blood gushed from his face.

Michael had recovered and was reaching for her, so she rammed a knee up into his crotch. He doubled over, howling. She kicked him in the chest.

She had just a few seconds before they would be on her again, so she lunged for the door, but she wasn't quick enough. The fight had woken the other vampires, and they emerged from all over the house. Quick as a flash, they descended on her, grabbing her arms, her legs, lifting her up off the ground.

She hung in the air, her body drawn in four directions as half a dozen vampires looked down at her with malice. She tensed, expecting them to rip her apart. Instead, they hauled her back downstairs, jostling her and pulling her joints out of socket as they moved, their steps out of sync.

Pain shot through her body as they jerked and tugged at her, and tears welled up in her eyes and dripped off her cheeks. Her breaths came fast, shallow, erratic, till she felt like she wasn't getting any oxygen at all.

They turned the locks and pulled open the door to her prison. Serena rushed out, gawking at Caroline, her face contorted with anger and disbelief. Caroline knew Serena was never on her side, but she'd been kind to her, at least, bringing her food and water and letting her shower. Caroline felt like she'd betrayed her only ally. But unless Serena was willing to help her escape, she was her enemy.

The vampires tossed her carelessly into the room. She supposed she should be grateful she landed on the mattress and not the concrete floor. They backed away as Michael walked in, holding the gun in one hand and a cell phone in the other. He looked calm on the outside, but she could see his anger simmering below the surface. Caroline flinched when he loomed over her, but he didn't touch her.

"I think we should let Roric know how eager you are to be released. Perhaps that will motivate him to accept my offer. And I'm sure he'd love to her from you." Michael tapped at the phone.

Caroline's body tensed with conflicting emotions. As much as she wanted to hear Roric's voice and tell him she was okay, she knew seeing her would only make him more likely to give in. As desperate as she was to be free, she couldn't let him give them what they wanted just to save her. She was only one person, but the Agency was protecting the whole city. And the city needed it more than ever. If she had to, she was willing to sacrifice her life to save others, and she needed Roric to accept that.

"He's not going to change his mind. The Agency is too important for him to give up."

Michael looked up from his phone. "You think he cares more about the Agency than he does about you, yet you're willing to mate with him?"

"No, but if I talk to him, I'll tell him not to give in to you. The Agency is more important than any one person."

"I see you're just as noble and committed to the cause as he is. But how will you feel when I fill your body with silver? Let's hope the sight of you writhing in pain will be enough to change Roric's mind." Michael smiled maliciously and tapped at the phone again.

CHAPTER FOURTEEN

The sun flared above the horizon, painting the sky and filling Roric's cruiser with pink and orange light. Too bad he couldn't appreciate the beauty. All it did was remind him how ugly the rest of the world was. Any other day, he'd be heading home now to get some sleep, but today he was wide awake, wired on gallons of liquid caffeine and anxiety that had his body humming with nervous energy. He approached the drive to his family's mansion, but he had no intention of stopping.

He'd collapsed for a little while yesterday after his rage-inducing phone call with Michael. Fear, anger, helplessness, and exhaustion had brought him to his knees. Taven told him he needed to get some sleep or he wouldn't have the energy to pursue it when they got another lead, and since he had no idea what to do next, he took his brother's advice and let himself crash for a few hours.

Now he was revived and reenergized, but he still had nothing to go on, so he drove around aimlessly, waiting for a sign to come from heaven, or something. Instead, it came in the form of a video call.

Roric grabbed the phone out of the center console at the first ring. As soon as he saw the name on the screen, he slammed on the brakes and swerved into the driveway then put the car in park and jabbed at the button to accept the call.

A face appeared on the screen that he didn't recognize, surrounded by several others. He recognized the voice, though, and it sent chills up and down his body, even though the man only said two words. "Hello, Roric."

"Michael," he sneered out the name, the only thing he knew about the vamp, and even that was probably fake. If he had something, anything else, he might've been able to search for him, but he had nothing. He took a screenshot hoping maybe somebody could help him identify his enemy.

"Have you reconsidered my offer?" The guy's voice was lilting, musical, almost like he was singing. It made Roric want to rip his vocal cords out.

"If I had, I would've called you. But you called me, so have you reconsidered mine?"

Michael chuckled like a goddamn wind chime, his blue eyes sparkling like the Caribbean Sea. "No, but I wanted to give you a little update. Your girlfriend is quite a spitfire. She managed to procure a stake, escape from a locked room, detain one of my cohorts, sneak past another, and walk right out of my house."

Roric's eyes bugged out and his mouth fell open as he barked out a laugh. That sounded like Caroline, alright. God, he loved her so much. She was incredible. She didn't even need him to save her.

"Don't get too excited. The story doesn't have the happy ending you imagine. She was moments from escaping when, thanks to fortuitous timing, I was able to apprehend her. She's back in her cell now, only slightly worse for wear."

Roric's hand clutched the steering wheel tight enough to mangle it, and his face twisted in a snarl. "What did you do to her? I want to see her."

"Yes, I thought you might. Thus the video call." Michael turned the phone around, and Caroline's face came into view.

Roric's heart inflated at the sight of her, like a helium balloon trying to escape his chest. He held it down with his hand. It lodged in his throat, instead, blocking off his voice and his air flow.

She was whole, and well, and alive. She looked better than the last time he saw her. Her hair was mussed, but her face and clothes were clean, and he didn't see any blood or signs of injury. His stomach clenched when he recognized the tee shirt she was wearing. It was one of his. He hoped it made her feel like he was with her, holding her.

"Caroline." He croaked out her name then pressed a fist to his mouth as tears welled up in his eyes.

Michael handed the phone to Caroline but pressed a gun to her head. He didn't say anything, but the threat was obvious. Caroline flinched a little then adjusted the phone so Roric couldn't see the muzzle.

"I'm coming for you, baby. I'm gonna find you. Just wait for me." He didn't want her to risk trying to escape again, even though he was proud of her for trying. He doubted she'd get another chance, anyway. Michael wouldn't underestimate her again.

"Roric, don't give in to him. The Agency is more important than anything else."

Michael yanked the phone away from her but kept it facing her. "So selfless. So devoted to the ridiculous notion that humans should rule over vampires. You two are a perfect match, aren't you? It's no wonder you're with her, even though she's not your normal type. Perhaps I need to up the stakes a little."

Suddenly, a loud bang blast through the phone speakers. The phone jostled, and when it stopped moving and focused on Caroline again, she was sprawled on a mattress, wailing, writhing in pain, and blood was darkening her tee shirt.

Roric roared as he felt the bullet pierce his own body and tear through the muscles, searing them with the acid burn of silver. Only, it felt like a hundred shots and not just one. His whole body contorted with agony at the thought of her suffering.

But Michael wasn't done. He shot her again and again, in the leg, the arm, the stomach. The only place he didn't shoot her was the head. She screamed and convulsed as each bullet exploded through her body. They ricocheted into Roric till his body was riddled with holes like a cheese grater. He slumped down, too weak to support his own weight. The black interior of the cruiser closed in on him like a grave. It might as well be. He felt like he'd died a dozen deaths, one for each shot.

Michael kept the phone facing Caroline so Roric could watch her body flail as it tried to expel the poisonous silver. She flopped around like an epileptic having a grand mal seizure. Roric almost wished Michael had shot her in the head so she wouldn't be conscious right now.

"You have one day left to save your precious mate, Roric. If you haven't shut down the Agency by then, you'll lose her and it. I won't hesitate to blow her brains out and ash her. Such a shame, because she's a keeper, isn't she? Smart, strong, beautiful. Is she tasty? Maybe I'll see for myself. Maybe I'll sink my fangs and my dick in her."

Roric howled at him, his body exploding with energy again. "Don't you touch her!"

"Be quick then. She'll be healed soon, and I'm not sure I'll be able to resist her." Michael reached out and stroked Caroline's hair, and rage detonated in Roric again.

"I'm going to find you, Michael. And when I do, I won't have any mercy. I already killed Derrick and Layla. I won't hesitate to kill you and all your henchmen. This is my town, and I don't intend to let some maniac destroy it!"

He hung up then, needing to feel some kind of control. His body vibrated with trapped energy like an earthquake, shaking the cruiser. He needed to do something, but what? He had no leads, no clue where to look for her.

Maybe it was time to give up. Not on Caroline but on the Agency. Maybe he needed to accept the fact that the rogues were taking over. He couldn't stop them, no matter how hard he tried. The rebellion just kept getting bigger and bigger. They'd bombed the school; what would they go after next? Would they start attacking human schools, government buildings? He was surprised they hadn't bombed the Agency yet.

But if Roric shut down the Agency, things would only get worse. There'd be no one to stop them from taking over. The human authorities were no match for vampires. They really would rule the world.

Maybe Roric should give them what they want, get Caroline, and run away from it all. Why did he have to be responsible for saving the world? He was only one vampire with a handful of agents, fighting against a rapidly growing army, and he was failing.

He was just about to drive to the news station and tell them he had an announcement to make when a car pulled into the driveway behind him, blocking him. Roric scowled at the yellow convertible in his rearview mirror. The redhead inside got out and headed towards his cruiser. He rolled down his window.

Piper's freckled nose wrinkled with worry. "Hey, Roric. I've been trying to reach Caroline ever since the bombing, but I can't get ahold of her. Please tell me she's okay."

Roric scrubbed his face with his hands. What should he say to her? Should he tell her the truth? There was no reason not to, other than the fact that it would upset her. But knowing Piper, she wouldn't let it go till she'd pestered the whole story out of him.

Roric sighed and climbed out of the car, sticking a hat on his head. He knew Piper was going to freak out and would probably need a hug or something. "She was kidnapped by the rogues right after the blast. They want me to shut down the school and the Agency."

Piper gawked at him and sputtered out several nonsense syllables before a few real words came out. "Oh my God, Roric! You must be freaking out right now!"

Sure enough, she threw herself at him, wrapping her tiny arms around his middle, but she was trying to comfort him, not the other way around. He stiffened at first, but then his body slumped into hers. He didn't realize how much he needed it.

His brother wasn't the type to give him a hug, and neither was his father. Since his mother died, Caroline was the only person who ever touched him like that. Roric put his arms around Piper and stroked her gently, amazed at how good it felt. Not in a sexual way, but like hugging a mother or a sister.

When she finally loosened her grip on him, he dropped his arms reluctantly. Tears stung his eyes, and his rubbed at them with his fists. Piper swiped hers off her cheeks with her fingertips.

"Have they let you talk to her? Is she okay?"

Roric's face scrunched up, and he clenched his teeth together to keep himself from having a breakdown. "I just got off the phone with the rogue leader, Michael. He let me talk to her for a minute. She's alive... for now. He gave me one more day to do what he wants, then he's going to kill her."

He couldn't bring himself to admit that he'd watched Michael pepper Caroline's body with silver bullets. Besides, that would only upset Piper unnecessarily. She couldn't help Caroline any more than Roric could.

"What are you going to do?"

He shook his head and stared off into the brightening horizon, too ashamed to make eye contact. "I've been trying to find her, but I'm out of leads. I don't know what else to do but give in to their demands."

"Have you questioned any of the rogues you have in custody? Maybe one of them can tell you something useful."

"I already interrogated the guy who told me they had Caroline. That's how I learned who their leader was. I didn't even know they had one. But neither he nor his creator knew how to find the guy. I questioned the others this morning, but none of them gave me anything useful."

Roric cringed, feeling like such a fool. He was the leader of the Agency, and yet he was totally ignorant when it came to his enemy. Maybe he needed to resign and let someone better take over.

"You should talk to Houston. He probably still has some feelings for Caroline, even though she staked him." The look on Piper's face made Roric think she might have some feelings for Houston too, but he didn't have the time to think about that right then.

He grabbed her arms, jolting her, then quickly let go, a huge smile stretching his face. "You're amazing, Piper. Why didn't I think of that? I've got to go, I've got a rogue to question."

He turned around and yanked his car door open then slid into the seat. He revved the engine, eager for Piper to get out of his way so he could get moving, but instead, she leaned into his window.

"Can I go with you? He might be more willing to talk if I'm there. We're… friends."

Roric raised an eyebrow at her, more questions bubbling to the surface. "Okay. Follow me to the prison."

Piper nodded eagerly then scurried back to her car and backed out of the driveway and down the road a few yards. Roric backed out in front of her then took off, lights and siren blazing. To her credit, Piper managed to keep up with him.

CHAPTER FIFTEEN

Her little Beetle whined and shimmied as Piper pressed the gas pedal to the floor, trying to keep up with Roric. She thought she might be able to run faster than her car was going. She was pretty sure her heart was revving faster than the engine. She wasn't sure if it was anxiety about Caroline, the thrill of adventure, or the thought of seeing Houston again, but whatever it was, it was like a drug coursing through her system, making her feel like she could fly. It was a way better rush than the pot of coffee she'd downed, trying to get her body back on school time after a couple months of summer vacation.

But thankfully, Roric had the lights and siren on, and she was following in his wake, so she didn't have to stop every time they came to an intersection. He was getting ahead of her, but not so much that she couldn't follow him. When she took a corner too fast, her car tilted so much, so thought it was going to flip over like they did in the movies. But instead, her wheels just squealed loudly, and her car skidded a little as it fishtailed before righting itself again.

Piper turned up the radio when a fast song came on and thumped her hands on the steering wheel in time to the music, grinning and belting out the lyrics. But when the song ended and a commercial came on, talking about back-to-school shopping, reality smacked her in the face like a bucket of water. Crap! She was supposed to be at work in a few minutes!

That was why she was up at the butt crack of dawn instead of sleeping in till 10 like she had been all summer. She was so worried she wouldn't be able to get up on time, she'd set her alarm an hour earlier than necessary, just in case. But she'd managed to get ready with a little time to spare, so she'd decided to stop by Roric's place to see if she could catch Caroline.

School hadn't started yet, it was just a teacher work-day, but she was still expected to be there. But there was no way on God's green earth that she was going to miss this opportunity. Her friend had been kidnapped, for heaven's sake, and the Agency needed her help to find her. If that wasn't a good reason to call in, she didn't know what was.

She reached for her phone, but Roric took another fast turn, and she scrambled for the steering wheel. Maybe she should wait till they got there. She'd never been to the prison before, but she knew it wasn't that far out of town.

She couldn't wrap her head around the idea that Caroline had been kidnapped. Although, it shouldn't surprise her, what with Caroline dating the leader of the Agency and the rogues hellbent on taking it down. She felt terrible that she'd been going about her life while her friend was in mortal danger.

But now that she knew, she was going to do everything

in her power to help. Not that there was much she could do. She was still a weak, powerless human. Just one more reason why she wished she was a vampire.

She was so tempted to take Davede up on his offer to change her, especially since she discovered that her feelings for him were stronger than she realized. But the fact that she was stoked to see Houston again was a big, flashing, warning sign, reminding her why she'd been hesitant in the first place.

She might have feelings for Davede, but they weren't strong enough to satisfy her. She wanted to be a vampire because it was exciting, and she craved the thrill of new experiences. But Davede wanted someone to settle down with. Settling down was the last thing she wanted to do.

When Piper pulled into the parking lot of the Wilburn County Penitentiary behind Roric, all other thoughts disappeared at the sight of the large, stone building surrounded by layers of razor wire-topped fencing. A guard tower stood in the corner, and Piper imagined a sniper looking down on them with a laser-sighted assault rifle. A shiver ran through her body as her excitement went cold with fear.

She grabbed her phone and jumped out of the car, waving it at Roric. "I need to make a quick call into work."

He nodded and started pacing back and forth beside his cruiser while she dialed the school. Suddenly, he whipped around to look at her. "Don't tell them what's going on. I don't want anyone knowing about Caroline."

Piper's mouth opened, but her words caught in her throat. How was she supposed to explain the importance of her absence if she couldn't tell them her friend had been kidnapped? When the secretary answered, Piper quickly made up a story about car trouble that sounded totally lame, but the secretary didn't act suspicious, so hopefully she bought it.

Piper hung up, stuck the phone in her back pocket, and hurried over to Roric with an eager smile on her face. "Okay, I'm ready. Let's do this!"

Roric frowned at her. "Keep your mouth shut till I tell you to talk, okay?"

Piper scowled at him and opened her mouth to complain, but then she clamped it shut again. She didn't want to give him any reason to tell her she couldn't come with him. And okay, so maybe she did have a big mouth. She thought it was part of her charm. Maybe Roric saw it differently.

She followed him up to the building then through more security checks than the White House or the Franklin Mint. She'd never been to a prison before, so she didn't know if that was normal or not, but the place was locked down tight. Maybe because it had more vampire inmates than any other prison in the country since it was so close to Modesa, the vampire capitol of America.

Roric's Agency shield got him through the security pretty quickly, and it was probably a lot easier for Piper since she was with him than it would've been otherwise. Still, she expected a cavity search any minute. Thank God they didn't require that. She shuddered just thinking about it.

Finally, the guard led them into a concrete block interrogation room with a heavy table, three folding chairs, and a two-way mirror on the wall. The room seemed awfully small and intimate compared with all the security that kept them separated from the prisoners. If she didn't know the inmate they were there to see, she'd feel really intimidated, being that close to a dangerous criminal.

She still couldn't think of Houston that way, even though technically he kind of was. He associated with the rebellion, drank from humans, and even attacked Caroline when she'd tried to call Roric to break up a party full of rogues. Maybe he'd look different to her now that he was a convicted felon. When the guards brought him in, wearing an orange jumpsuit, shuffling because his hands and ankles were shackled, Piper stared at him for a moment, trying to reconcile the man in front of her with the fun-loving guy she used to fool around with.

But then his face broke open in a wide smile, and he flicked his golden blond hair out of his whiskey brown eyes and stared at her. "Piper."

She grinned back at him. God, he was cute. And he was still Houston. Roric scowled at him, but Houston ignored him.

She wanted to grab ahold of him and hug him, but the guard pushed him down into one of the chairs and cuffed his hands to the table. Roric pulled out a chair for her then sat down in the other one. Piper sat down and slid her hands across the table, automatically reaching for him, but Roric pulled her arms back at the same time the guard barked out, "No touching."

Piper put her hands in her lap so she wouldn't be tempted again. "Hey, Houston. How are you doing? You look good."

"Well, I'm in prison, so I'm kind of terrible. But it sure is good to see you again. You look amazing. Thanks for coming to see me." Her cheeks pinked as his eyes roved up and down her body.

She glanced down at her outfit and cringed. If she'd known ahead of time that she was coming here, she might've dressed a little differently. She was wearing her school teacher business casual look — khaki slacks with a fitted, blue, button-down shirt. Davede must be rubbing off on her. But Houston didn't seem to mind her boring outfit. He stared at her for another long moment, his eyes flashing like his mind was playing back memories of their time together and thinking about all the things he'd like to do with her now.

Roric cleared his throat, and Houston tore his gaze away from her to look at him. "We're not here for you two to catch up. I need you to tell me everything you know about a rogue named Michael."

Houston stiffened and pulled back, and his eyes got big. "I don't know anybody named Michael."

Roric slammed a fist on the table, jostling it even though it weighed a ton. Piper flinched. She always forgot how strong vampires were because the ones she hung around were always so careful with her. But Roric could probably put a hole in the table if he wanted to. It was pretty amazing that they could control their strength the way they did. Her mind started to wander off in a fantasies of what she would do if she were that strong, but Roric's words snapped her back to the present.

"The way you just reacted tells me you know exactly who I'm talking about, so start talking."

Houston screwed up his face in a scowl and moved his hands like he wanted to cross his arms over his chest, but the cuffs stopped him. He let his arms drop to the table again, the shackles rattling loudly agains the metal. It sent a chill through Piper, reminding her that he wasn't the sweet, innocent guy she thought he was. "So what if I do know something. Why would I tell you?"

Roric leaned forward and snarled. "I already have a grudge against you for what you did to Caroline. I wouldn't test me if I were you."

"Yeah, well, I'll be a dead man if the rogues in here think I'm giving up information to the Agency, so I'll take my chances." A look of fear crossed Houston's face, and Piper gasped, imagining what kinds of terrible things might happen to him.

Roric scrubbed his face with his hand and sighed. "What do you want, Houston? Name your price."

Houston didn't hesitate. "I want out of here. Today."

Roric shook his head. "You know I can't do that."

"In the next month, then. Before I starve to death in here." Houston tried to sound tough, but the way his voice wobbled, Piper could tell it was a bigger deal than he was willing to admit.

Prisons weren't required to provide blood for vampires, so they had to rely on friends or family to supply them if their sentence was longer than they could survive without it. As far as Piper knew, Houston wasn't that close to any other vampires, and he'd been in jail for several months. How long could he go without blood?

"I'll feed him," Piper blurted out.

She quickly turned away to look at Houston. "If you tell Roric everything you know."

Roric gawked at her. "What, like a conjugal visit? Piper, you don't have to do that."

"I don't mind. We've... done it before." She dropped her head. The way Roric was acting, he obviously didn't know she and Houston had that kind of relationship.

137

Would he think less of her? She didn't care. It was the only thing she could do to help.

"I'd do anything to help Caroline." As soon as the words were out, she slapped a hand over her mouth, but it was too late.

Houston jerked. "What's wrong with Caroline?"

Piper mouthed, "I'm sorry," and held her hand up to her face to cover her cringe as she looked at Roric.

Roric grimaced. "She's in trouble; that's all you need to know. Do we have a deal?"

Houston gave Piper a quick glance then nodded. "Michael is the leader of the rebellion. He's got dozens of rogues under him who do whatever he says."

"Where can I find him?"

"He's got a place out on Banshee Road. The big, old farmhouse."

Roric sat up straighter with an eager look on his face and pulled a small notepad and pen out of his back pocket then tossed it on the table. "You been there? I need to know everything about it. Can you draw the layout?"

Houston shook his head. "No, that's just what I've heard."

Roric's face fell, and he pounded the table again, making the pen bounce and roll onto the ground. "Damn. I need to get in there."

"Well, you better take your whole crew with you. Several high-level rogues live there with him. The place is probably under watch 24-7."

Roric's face twisted with anxiety, and Houston gave Piper a questioning look, but she kept her mouth shut that time. He turned towards Roric. "What does this have to do with Caroline?"

Roric pressed his palms together in front of his lips then scrubbed his hands up and down his face. "He has her, and he's going to kill her if I don't get her out of there by tomorrow."

Houston sat dead silent like he hadn't heard a word that Roric said, but the look on his face told Piper he knew something and it was tearing him up inside. She reached out a hand to touch him but stopped an inch away, glancing at the guard in the corner.

"Please, Houston. You have to help us. Tell us anything you know. I'll come feed you every week if you want me to."

"The higher-ups have a meeting every week at Michael's place, on Monday nights. I heard a rumor that they're planning another attack. Tons of rogues will be there."

"Shit. That's tonight. There's not enough time." Roric jumped up, knocking over his chair. It clattered to the concrete. He leaned over and glared at Houston. "You know anything else?"

Houston shook his head. Roric turned towards Piper. "I gotta go. Take care of him."

He walked out, leaving Piper alone with Houston. Houston stared at her for a long moment before speaking. "It's really good to see you again. Sorry it has to be under these circumstances."

She gave him a small smile. "Me too. But thank you for helping. It means a lot."

He nodded and stared at her a little more. "So, what have you been up to? Anything new in your life?"

Piper shrugged. She had a feeling it was more than just small talk, that he was feeling her out to see where they stood. But she didn't know either. She still liked him, but things were definitely different now.

"Today was supposed to be my first day back to school, but then this came up."

Houston grinned and dropped his head. "You gonna tell your students you visited a convicted rogue in prison?"

She laughed. "Definitely not. So, um, do we do this here, or what?" She blushed and fiddled nervously with the collar of her shirt, anxious to get it over with now.

Houston winced and shook his head, the sparkle in his eyes dulling like watered-down whiskey. "No, the guard will take us to a private feeding room. Are you sure you're okay with this? I don't want you to have to do anything you're not comfortable with."

She forced a smile and stood up. "No, it's fine. It's no big deal."

Houston's lip and brow bunched up, and he stared at the table. "Yeah, it's just a meal, right?"

The guard unshackled Houston from the table and led them out of the interrogation room and into a room without a table and a two-way mirror. There was a full-size bed and a couple upholstered chairs, but the concrete walls and floor and exposed sink and toilet made it feel like a prison cell.

"You got 30 minutes." The guard took Houston's cuffs off then locked the door behind them.

Houston immediately reached for her, and Piper stiffened. She didn't know why she felt so uncomfortable. This was Houston. She'd been with him several times, and it was always amazing.

He stroked a hand gently down her neck. "I missed you, Piper. I thought about you all the time, imagining this.

But I can tell you're not into this."

It was good to see him again, but he didn't have the same effect on her as he used to. Was it because he was off-limits till he got out of prison, or was it because of Davede? She wasn't sure, but she knew there was nothing left between them. Still, she felt uncomfortable telling him about Davede, but she owed it to both of them.

"I think I'm in love with someone else."

CHAPTER SIXTEEN

Roric's first instinct was to drive to the farmhouse on Banshee Road and bust in there with guns blazing to rescue Caroline. He spent the first half of the drive back to town imagining himself going in there like the Terminator, destroying everything in his wake.

But the drive was long enough that he also had enough time to imagine how it might turn out, and no matter how he pictured it, it always ended the same way. Badly.

By the time he got back to Modesa, the rational side of his brain had managed to convince the superhero side that he was doomed to fail if he didn't come up with a better plan first. He pulled out his phone and called an emergency meeting at the Agency with his most trusted agents.

When he turned into the parking lot, he was relieved to see a line of cruisers and even Raven's sleek sedan waiting for him. She was a little too soft, wanting to believe that most newly-turned vampires were innocent victims instead of dangerous rogues, but she'd provide a counterbalance if the testosterone level got out of control.

Inside, Veena had the coffee going, perfuming the air with the re-energizing scent of dark roast. They were gonna need it. It was way past bedtime for most of them, and they wouldn't get much chance to sleep before they had to put the plan into action. But first they had to figure out the plan.

Roric tromped down the hall to the briefing room, poured himself a cup of joe, black, and downed it in one gulp. Then he turned to face the room full of muttering agents. Their stares followed him as he moved to the front of the room and stood behind the podium, his hands curling tight around the worn wood.

"As most of you know, my girlfriend, Caroline, was kidnapped from my home after the grand opening Saturday night and is being held hostage by a group of rogues. I've been in contact with the leader, Michael. He wants me to close the Agency and the school and announce to the public that vampires will no longer comply with the terms of the treaty. I have till the end of the day."

The few agents who hadn't heard the story gasped and started looking at each other and whispering. Raven's face twisted up in sympathy. But Roric kept talking before they had a chance to ask any questions.

"Obviously, I refused his demands. My brother and I and several of you have been combing the streets, searching for any information about where they might be hiding her, but we didn't have any good leads... until today."

"I spoke with a rogue prisoner today who told me that Michael has a farmhouse out on Banshee Road, and the rogues have a meeting there every Monday night." More whispers from the group.

"They're planning another attack." The room went

dead silent.

"I don't know yet what their next target is, but since I've made no attempts to agree to Michael's terms, it wouldn't surprise me if it was the Agency. That means we need to be proactive if the Agency is going to survive. I'm a little too close to this, so I want to hear your thoughts."

Taven jumped up. "This is perfect. All the high-level rogues in one place at one time. I say we launch a full-on attack. Steal a page from their own book and drop a bomb on them, take them all down at once."

Raven glared at Taven, putting her hands on her slim hips and tossing her sharp bob. "You can't do that! Not without reasonable cause. We're law enforcement, not vigilantes."

Taven sneered at her. "They gave us reasonable cause when they blew up your school, remember?"

She rolled her eyes at him and smoothed a hand down her fitted suit. Roric wondered if she slept in one of those. "Of course I remember. I worked my butt off on that school, and now the opening is delayed by weeks if not months. But you have no proof that this Michael person set that bomb. There's a system of justice, procedures we need to follow. If we act with impunity, how are we any different from the rogues? Right, Roric?"

She glanced at him, obviously expecting him to back her up, and normally he would. He believed in the law, believed in due process and the justice system, and he always tried to do the right thing, be the kind of vampire the world could trust. But when it came to Caroline, the rules always seemed to go right out the window. He'd do anything to get her back, even if it meant rejecting everything else he believed in.

POSSESSED BY THE VAMPIRE

He shook his head at her, a grave look on his face. "We're past the point of playing by the rules, Raven. If we wait till we have proof in hand, the rogues will destroy everything we're trying to save. We can't afford to miss this opportunity. Besides, they took Caroline, and that's a big enough crime to warrant an attack in my mind. But I'll admit, my judgement is clouded right now. What do the rest of you think?"

He looked around the room at his most devoted agents, the vampires who'd worked with him for the last few years, trying to manage the growing problem by chasing down one rogue at a time.

Markus, one of his senior agents, spoke up, reiterating what Roric was thinking. "What we've been doing isn't working. The rogues have upped their game from random, individual crimes to planned attacks, and we need to step up ours. I don't think anybody is going to be upset if we go in there and blast them all, except for the rogues."

The other agents all started talking at once, but everyone seemed to have the same opinion. The only person with any reservations was Raven, but she wouldn't be involved in the operation, anyway, so it really didn't matter if she agreed with it. And she didn't have any better ideas.

Roric knocked a few times on the podium to get everyone to quiet down for a minute. "Okay, so I think we're all in agreement. We'll take advantage of their meeting tonight to take them down before their next attack. I like Taven's idea of a bomb. It will kill a lot of birds with one stone, and it'll be poetic justice. Leven, do you think you can make something for us by tonight?"

Leven, an agent with an engineering degree and an

obsession with explosives, nodded and gave a wry smile, pushing up his thick, black-rimmed glasses. "Are you kidding? I've got half a dozen devices in my basement, all ready to go. I've just been waiting for the opportunity to use one of them."

Roric smirked and shook his head. "I should probably be worried about that, but right now I'm just grateful. Okay, next step. We need to get the bomb inside, hide it, and rig it to go off without anyone noticing. How are we going to do that?"

"I've got a device small enough for one person to carry in. If we wait till they're all occupied with their meeting, we can probably sneak one agent in, set the bomb with a three minute timer, and get out before anyone notices," Leven said.

"Will it kill everyone?" Taven asked, a vicious gleam in his eyes. He'd sat back down, but his massive body was vibrating with excitement.

Leven tugged on his buttoned-up dress shirt collar. "It should obliterate everyone within a twenty-foot radius, so we'll have to put it close to the crowd."

"The rest of us can surround the property and take down anyone who escapes," another agent suggested.

Roric nodded and paced back and forth across the front of the room, endorphins building up in his bloodstream. "This sounds like a good plan, so far. There's only one problem. We need to find Caroline and get her out of there before we blast them. How are we going to do that?"

Taven frowned and crossed his arms over his chest. "If you go in there ahead of time and get caught, they're going to suspect that something's up. We'll lose our advantage. We can't risk it."

Roric gawked at him. What the hell was wrong with his brother? "Well, we sure as hell can't blow up the place if Caroline's still in there! We have to get her out first."

"I know you want to charge in there and rescue her, but if one rogue sees you, they'll know we're onto them. And there's no way you're getting in there without being seen. Even if you take down every rogue who crosses your path, they're gonna notice the dead bodies. Sorry, Roric, but it's not going to work."

The other agents started muttering, the tone of their voices telling him that they agreed with Taven. Roric stared at them, dumbfounded. How could they possibly expect him to blow up the building where the woman he loved was being held captive?

The others might not realize what Caroline meant to him since he'd kept their relationship on the down low, not wanting anyone to suspect that he'd been the one to turn Caroline. But his brother knew how close he and Caroline were. He knew that Roric had broken every rule just to be with her. How could he be so callous? What if it was Ivy, instead?

"Then the plan's off. I'm not sacrificing Caroline's life. No way." Roric cut his arms through the air in a motion of finality.

Taven jumped up and stomped towards the front, addressing the other agents as much as Roric. "This is our best chance to take them down. We can't waste this opportunity just to save one person. These rogues have killed dozens of people, and they're only going to kill more if we don't stop them."

The others seemed a little hesitant to agree, but Roric could see in their eyes that they did. He understood where they were coming from. It was their best chance to take down the rogues. They might never get another opportunity like this. But it wasn't their intended mate locked away in that house.

How could he do both — rescue Caroline and still take down the enemy? There had to be a way. Could he bribe a rogue to get Caroline out before the attack? He didn't know any rogues that he could even consider trusting. Even if he did, as soon as Caroline came up missing, Michael would know they'd found his hiding spot. If he was smart, he'd assume the worst and change his plans. The only way it could work was if they rescued Caroline right before the bomb went off.

A plan emerged in Roric's mind. It was crazy and dangerous, and there was absolutely no margin for error. If he failed, he and Caroline would both die. But it was the only thing that might work. If he didn't get Caroline out of there tonight, she'd be dead by tomorrow.

While Roric contemplated, the others started talking amongst themselves, strategizing. By the time he'd made up his mind, so had they. Everyone was in favor of bombing Michael's hideout that night.

Roric rapped on the podium to get their attention. It took a few moments for them to settle down. "Okay, we'll do it. Let's nail down the details."

CHAPTER SEVENTEEN

Caroline's body writhed on the filthy mattress, drenched in sweat and blood, as pain exploded from the bullet holes and streaked through every nerve ending. The silver burned the flesh it touched like acid and poisoned her bloodstream till every vein was on fire. Her body immediately started to push the bullets out at the same time her skin tried to close over them, making their exit just as excruciating as their entry.

She knew the bullets wouldn't kill her, but she was in so much pain, she wished they would. She was going to die, anyway. Michael would kill her if Roric didn't meet his demands. She had no doubt about that.

She hated that Roric had to see her being shot. She knew he was in almost as much agony as she was, knowing that she was being tortured because of him. And his controlling side was probably going berserk, not being able to do anything.

She didn't think Roric knew anything about Michael before then. How would he ever figure out where Michael was hiding her in time? He'd try his best, but the odds were, he wouldn't. She knew that. That was why she'd tried to save herself. It would've worked, too, if Michael hadn't chosen that exact moment to return. She'd done her best; it just wasn't enough.

Michael shoved the gun in the back of his pants and sneered down at her with no sign of sympathy or remorse as her body reacted to the gunshot wounds. "Learn this lesson, Caroline. I believe in every vampire for himself. In that, I admire your attempt to free yourself. You're strong-willed, and I like that. If I could convince you to see things my way, I'd keep you for myself."

Caroline's stomach rolled as he leered at her. She'd heard his comment to Roric about sinking his fangs in her. It made her sick to think about his hot breath on her neck, his lips drawing the blood from her veins. She hated that her blood was spilling out for him now, tempting him.

"But I can't trust you. Despite his unwillingness to sacrifice for you, you still love him, don't you? Pathetic. If he truly loved you, he'd give up anything to save you. But he cares more about the Agency than he does you."

The words hurt almost as much as the bullet wounds. She clutched her chest, trying to ease the pain. She tried to remind herself that she wanted Roric to stand up to Michael, but it still felt like a stake to her heart that he could sacrifice her, even if it was the right thing to do.

Michael backed away from her, like he'd already written her off in his mind. "I have no mercy for anyone who interferes with my plans. Since Roric won't get out of my way, I'll take him down, and the rest of the Agency with him. I'm looking forward to it. He'll die for what he loves, it just won't be you."

Serena's boyfriend, Leon, looked from Caroline to

Michael. "Yo, Michael. Can I be the one to kill her? I'd like to make it up to my girlfriend."

Michael glared at him. "Your girlfriend is weak. She let her feelings get in the way of the mission and look what happened! I ought to kill her, too."

He whipped his gun out and swung it towards Serena. She gasped and threw her hands up to her chest, covering the ragged hole in her blouse where the stake had been.

"But I think it will be more poetic to have Serena kill Caroline. It will teach her a lesson and rub it in Roric's face that his own secretary turned on him and killed his woman. In the meantime, you'll keep an eye on her while we have our meeting. If she escapes again, then I'll let Leon take care of you." He gave an evil smile, and Leon gulped and gave Serena a warning glare.

Michael walked out of the room, and the other vampires followed him, leaving Caroline alone in the room with Serena. Serena looked horrified. She stood in the corner, wringing her hands and glancing guiltily at Caroline.

"I'm sorry I staked you. I didn't want to hurt you. Thank you for being kind to me." Caroline managed to gasp out the words even though her throat burned.

Serena moved closer, grabbing the water bottle she'd brought earlier and holding it up to Caroline's mouth. "I don't want to kill you, but I have no choice. If I don't, Michael will kill us both."

Caroline choked a little but then managed to swallow some of the cool, clean water. It felt like heaven on her flaming body. She wished she could douse herself with it.

She wanted to beg Serena to help her escape, but at this point, it was more important that she convince her to help Roric stop the rogues from attacking the Agency.

Caroline looked Serena in the eye, trying to draw out the compassion she knew was buried inside. "He's going to kill Roric and all the other agents. Are you going to stand by and watch him do it? Don't you care about them at all? They were your coworkers, your friends. Do you really love Leon enough to let all of them die?"

Serena shook her head. "I can't stop him even if I wanted to. I'm just one person."

"Maybe not, but you can warn Roric. Tell him what they have planned so he can be prepared." Caroline squinted as a bead of sweat rolled down her forehead and into her eyes, stinging her. She didn't have the strength to wipe it away.

"I don't know what they have planned. They're going to discuss it tonight at their meeting." Serena wiped Caroline's brow with the sheet.

"So go to the meeting and find out."

"I'm supposed to stay here and guard you." Serena gave her a conflicted look.

"I'm not going anywhere." Caroline cried out and writhed as one of the shallower bullets tore through the closed-over flesh and fell from her body. There were still a dozen more to go. Even once they were all out, she expected she'd be too weak to move for quite some time.

Serena looked at her bloody, bullet-riddled body and came to the same conclusion. "Okay, I'll try to eavesdrop on them, but I'm not making any promises."

Caroline hoped that hearing their plan would be enough to motivate Serena to act. She wasn't a rogue at heart, she was just desperate for attention and got drawn in to the wrong crowd. "You're a good person, Serena. I

154

believe you'll do the right thing."

Serena gulped and nodded. "I'm gonna go get a bucket of water and a rag to clean you up. I'll be right back."

She spent the next few hours by Caroline's side, washing the blood off her body and holding her hand when the pain got worse as the deeper bullets pushed their way out through thick layers of flesh. Eventually, all the bullets came out, and her wounds healed over. Caroline was exhausted, but the only pain left was a dull ache from the silver poisoning. She finally fell asleep late in the afternoon.

She woke up a few hours later to Serena shaking her. "Caroline, the meeting is about to start. They have guards watching the doors. I don't know how you could get past them, but I'm going to leave the door unlocked for you. I'm going to listen in on the meeting, then I'll go tell Roric what they have planned."

She slipped out without waiting for Caroline to respond, leaving Caroline's makeshift stake beside the bed. She shut the door behind her, but she didn't engage the deadbolts. Caroline stared at the closed door, trying to decide what to do.

If she stayed, Michael would definitely kill her. If she tried to escape, she'd have to take down at least one guard, maybe more, and she doubted she was strong enough to do it. If they caught her, Michael would blame Serena and maybe kill her before she had a chance to get to Roric.

Caroline hauled herself up off the mattress to see if her legs would hold her. They were weak and shaky. So were her arms when she practiced swinging the stake. There was no way she could defend herself. But could she manage to

POSSESSED BY THE VAMPIRE
sneak out without getting caught?

CHAPTER EIGHTEEN

The agents stood in a circle in the briefing room, looking at the small device sitting on one of the chairs. Roric guessed they were all secretly grateful they weren't the one who was tasked with infiltrating the rogue meeting and hiding it. The person who was assigned the life-threatening job seemed way too excited about it. Taven bounced on his heels, swinging his arms and pumping his fists like a boxer getting ready for a match.

Roric pulled him aside after Leven finished explaining how to set the bomb. "Hey man, you sure you're the right person for this job? You seem awfully worked up. I need you to keep a cool head."

Roric didn't really think Taven was the best choice for the job since he was more recognizable than some of the other agents and also because he was more of a "barge in and start a fight" type than a "sneak in and hide a bomb" kind of guy. But Taven had insisted he wanted to do it, and no one else was fighting him for the job.

"I'm good, I'm cool. I'm just looking forward to blasting some rogue ass." Taven threw a few fake jabs at

Roric.

"Yeah, well, don't get your own ass blasted in the process."

"I won't, but even if I do, at least I'll die a hero. It might be my only chance to outshine you." He gave a wry smile.

Roric frowned at him. "Is that why you volunteered? You want the glory? You don't have to risk your life for that. We're not in competition with each other."

Taven scowled at him and smacked a fist into his hand right in Roric's face. "Maybe you're not, because you've always been on top. Older, smarter, better at everything except maybe kicking ass. That's why Dad put you in charge of the Agency; you're the golden boy."

Roric shook his head. He hated that his brother had always felt that way, but he didn't know how to prove him otherwise. "Taven, that's not true. We just have different skills."

"Yeah? Well, one of mine is doing stupid things, so this is a perfect job for me. Besides, I got nothing to lose." Taven hid his pain behind a snarl, but Roric could see it.

"Well, Dad and I would lose a lot if we lost you. And what about Ivy?"

Taven suddenly got interested in the floor. He dropped his head and stared at it like he was counting the flecks in the tile. "Ivy and I are done."

"What? Since when?" Roric sat down on a nearby chair to show his brother he was there to listen. They didn't have too many heart to heart talks, they were guys, after all, but it sounded like Taven could use one. Even if his brother didn't want to admit it, Roric knew Taven was in love with Ivy.

"Since the night of the bombing." Taven plopped down next to him, their broad shoulders and widespread knees touching.

Roric felt like a jerk for not noticing what his brother was dealing with, but he'd been too busy dealing with his own drama. "What? No way. Ivy loves you."

Taven looked up, but not at Roric. Now a blank wall had his attention. "She got upset that I left to help you look for Caroline, and she went to the bar to hook up with another guy."

Roric sighed and put a hand on Taven's shoulder. "She was probably just trying to make you jealous. She got her own issues, you know. She's been abandoned by everyone who was supposed to care about her. She doesn't trust that you're going to stick around any more than you trust her."

Taven's face puckered up, and he raised an eyebrow. Had he really never realized that about Ivy? It was obvious to Roric. But maybe Taven was too blinded by his own insecurity to recognize anyone else's.

Taven winced and dropped his head again, suddenly fascinated by his hands. "I told her I never wanted a serious relationship."

Roric held in a snort and resisted the urge to tell him how stupid that was. "Is it true?"

"Yeah. No. Hell, I don't know. I can't risk getting that close to someone again and losing them. I don't know how you're functioning right now with the thought of losing Caroline."

Roric decided that was a pretty good segue for him to tell Taven about his crazy plan to rescue Caroline. "About as well as you're functioning. I'm about to do something batshit crazy. I'm going in there with you, and I'm gonna find Caroline and get her out before the bomb goes off."

Taven jumped up and gawked at him. "What the hell, bro? You'll have like five minutes, tops, before the place explodes. There's no way you're gonna find her and get her out of there in time. You're both gonna die."

Roric's face crumpled. He knew it was true, but having Taven say it out loud made it seem more real. "I have to try. I'll never be able to live with myself if I don't."

Taven barked out a harsh laugh. "Shit. We're both dead men."

Roric gave his own hollow laugh then grew serious again. "You should call Ivy. Tell her how you feel before we do this. What have you got to lose? If she doesn't want you, then you can take out your anger on the rogues. If she responds the way I think she will, it might give you a little more motivation to make it out alive."

"Yeah, maybe I will. Thanks, bro." Taven slugged him on the shoulder and walked away, pulling his phone out of his pocket.

Taven might have a jealous streak towards his brother, but in that moment, Roric had never envied Taven more. His woman was safe, and all he had to do to get her back was talk to her. Roric had to risk his life, and even then, there was no guarantee he'd get her out alive. He'd give anything to be able to call her right now and tell her how much he loved her. He'd tell her face to face, as soon as he got her out of there.

He jumped up, eager to get going and end this, one way or another. He went over the plan with his agents one more time, just to make sure they were all on the same page. Then he waited for Taven to come back.

When Taven returned, he had a look on his face that Roric couldn't quite decipher. He wanted to pull him aside and ask him, but the guys were all standing around, ready to go, and Taven hustled up to them and bellowed, "What are you pussies waiting for? Let's go blow up some vampires!"

They agents cheered and started heading out, Taven at the lead, so Roric let it drop. Taven would tell him when he was ready. For now, it looked like he was more interested in getting the show on the road.

They all took a back way out towards the farmhouse, staying off the main road so the rogues wouldn't see them approaching and parking their cruisers about half a mile away. Then the agents trekked through the dark woods on foot and took up hiding spots all around the farmhouse.

Roric hiked in with Taven. They walked silently for a few minutes, fallen leaves and broken tree branches crackling under their feet the only sound, but Roric couldn't staunch his curiosity for long. "So, you gonna tell me how it went or leave me hanging?"

Taven smirked at him. "It went... okay. We're gonna talk some more after this is over. She said she'll wait for me at the house."

Roric smiled, feeling a lot better now that Taven had a reason not to turn this into a suicide mission. "Hey, maybe when all this is over, we can have a joint mating ceremony, or something."

Taven just laughed and shook his head. They were close enough to the farmhouse that they needed to be quiet, so the conversation ended, but Roric let the idea play out in his head, forcing himself to believe that it was possible. It distracted him from his increasing heartbeat and the tension that was coiling up in his body, making his muscles tighten and the hair on his arms stand up.

When they got to the edge of the woods, they stopped and hid while they scoped out the farmhouse. Cars filled the front lawn, but Roric didn't see anyone walking around, so the meeting must have already started. There were no other houses close by, so the farmhouse was surrounded by darkness, but Roric's vampire eyesight made it easy enough for him to see through it. His agents were well-hidden. There was almost no movement in the muggy, late summer air, so he couldn't smell them, either.

A porch light lit up the front of the house, buzzing with gnats and shining a golden circle around a guard standing outside the door, leaning against the rickety porch railing. He glanced around occasionally, but he didn't look too worried about invaders. The back of the house wasn't lit up, but there was a vampire hanging out by the back door. Roric figured it would be easy enough to take him down if they could sneak up on him, but what would they find inside? Would more rogues be guarding the door from the inside? He hated going in blind, but he had no other option.

"Let's split up. I'll go over there and make some noise, try to distract the guard at the back door. Then you come up behind him," Taven suggested.

Roric nodded. It was as good a plan as any. Taven took off through the woods till he was a hundred feet away, then he started thrashing around like a wild animal tromping through the woods. Right away, the guard whipped his head towards the sound. Roric took the opportunity to dash towards the house and press himself up against the side. No one hollered at him or rushed to attack him, so he figured he hadn't been seen. He took a deep breath and held it, trying to hear over his racing heart.

Taven was deep enough that Roric couldn't see him in the dark green foliage, so the guard probably couldn't either, but Taven moved a little farther away, crashing through the woods as he went, and the guard's eyes followed the rustling tree branches.

Roric didn't waste a moment. He dashed around the corner of the house and pounced on the distracted guard's back, hurtling them both to the ground. He immediately shoved the guard's head into the grass to keep him from screaming. His gun dug into his side, tempting him to put a bullet in the vamp's head, but he couldn't risk the noise.

Instead, he shoved a stake through his back, aiming for his heart. The vampire went stiff under him, so he knew he'd hit the right spot. It made him appreciate all those hours he'd spend practicing his staking skills on a medical dummy.

No one came out to see where the guard had gone, so that gave Roric hope that security was minimal. Hopefully, most of the other rogues were in the meeting and he and Taven would be able to check out the place without interference. It was unlikely, but the rogues had an inflated sense of superiority, so maybe that led to a sense of infallibility, too.

Taven appeared beside him then, and together they carried the guard into the woods, leaving the stake in him. They both had holsters full of them, so they could afford to lose it. When this was all over, they'd come back and finish him off, or maybe just leave him for the sun to take care of.

After they dumped him, they hustled back up to the house and approached the back door from opposite sides with stakes drawn and ready to attack. Yellow light shone through the small window in the door, but a blind covered it. Roric slowly turned the knob then carefully opened the door a crack and waited with bated breath to see if there was any response. When nothing happened, he pressed his face to the door and peeked through the crack.

He couldn't see much, but he didn't see any vampires, so he quietly pushed the door open enough to slip through and found himself in an empty, high-end kitchen with new, solid maple cabinetry and travertine tile. Michael had fixed up the inside of the place while leaving the outside rundown, probably to ward off unwanted visitors. It made Roric more curious about the man, but if things went the way he hoped, he might never get any answers. But he'd get justice, and that was more important.

He turned back towards the door and waved at Taven who'd moved to the other side of the door. Taven slipped in beside him and glanced around at the room with the same look of curiosity that Roric had. They only had a moment to look around, though, before a vampire walked into the kitchen.

He didn't react to their presence at first, but then he did a double take and recognized them. Roric was on him before he had a chance to respond, shoving a stake in his chest with a wet thud that sounded loud to Roric but probably would go unnoticed. The vampire seized up, a shocked look on his face, his hands half-raised in a belated attempt at defense.

Taven pulled on a set of folding doors that opened to reveal a pantry. Roric lifted the guy up and shoved him in

164

the closet then shut the doors on him. Two down; how many more to go? Hopefully not too many, because it was time for him and Taven to split up.

Chills streaked up his spine when he heard Michael talking from a room in the distance. Taven needed to get as close as he could to plant the bomb, but Roric was almost positive that Caroline wouldn't be with the rogues. Michael had her locked up somewhere; Roric just had to find her and get her out. Neither job would be quick.

But it would only take a minute or two for Taven to do his job. Then he'd text Roric and get out of there. That would leave Roric with less than three minutes before the timer went off and the whole place exploded.

There was no time for Roric to agonize about it, though. Every moment they spent inside was another chance for them to be discovered. If anyone saw them and alerted the others, they'd never get a chance to do what they came for before they were surrounded.

Roric looked at Taven and nodded, and Taven took off towards the sound of Michael's voice. Roric went the other way. He peeked around a corner and saw a hallway with several doors leading off it. Going down it would leave him totally exposed, but he needed to check out those doors. He wished his stupid heart would stop pounding so he could hear better. All he could do was hope that everyone was occupied with the meeting and no one would be wandering around.

He slipped down the hallway and held his breath as he slowly cracked open the first door. The room beyond was dark, but he could make out a bed and a dresser. If he wanted to do this right, he'd investigate it anyway, even though it was an unlikely place for Caroline to be, but he didn't have time for that, so he moved on to the next room. Another dark bedroom.

No light shined under the third door, either, so he figured it was another bedroom, but he peeked inside, anyway. He jerked and almost yelped when he came face to face with a woman, hiding in the darkness. He immediately slapped a hand over her mouth so she couldn't scream, then pressed a stake to her chest, but he was hesitant to stake a woman, even if she was a rogue. Her eyes got wide, and her breath puffed hot and fast against his palm as he dug the stake deeper.

Something about her seemed familiar. He wanted to turn on the light and look at her, but he didn't have a free hand. "Make a sound, and I'll stake you before you get out more than one syllable."

He slowly pulled his hand away from her mouth and reached behind him to switch on the light when she didn't start yelling. The overhead turned on, filling the room with brightness, and Roric flinched at the sight of Serena.

"Holy shit, Serena. What the hell are you doing here?" he whispered. The last thing he wanted to do was stake his old secretary, but damnit, what choice did he have? She'd turned on him and sided with the enemy.

Her body quivered violently. "Roric, please don't hurt me. Caroline is here. I promised her I'd listen in on the meeting and come tell you what they were planning."

She sounded sincere, but he wasn't sure if he believed her. "Where is she?"

"She's in the basement. There aren't any other guards down there. I was supposed to be guarding her, but I left the door unlocked so she can try to escape if she wants. But she's really weak from the gunshots."

Roric's phone buzzed in his pocket, and his body immediately clenched like a coiled spring. He yanked the phone out and glanced at it, but he already knew what it would say. Taven had placed the bomb and set the timer. The final countdown had started.

Roric shoved the phone away and glared at Serena, pressing the stake harder against her chest. "Where's the basement?"

She gulped and pointed the direction he'd been going. "The next door down on the left. I'm... I'm sorry, Roric."

He nodded, but he didn't have time to talk. But her apology rang true, so before he opened the door, he said, "You need to get out of the house and leave now."

He didn't explain why, but at least he'd warned her. What she did with his warning was up to her.

He slipped out into the hallway and spotted the door to the basement. He was just about to turn the knob when a door opened across the hall and a rogue stepped out of the bathroom. Shit! Why hadn't he noticed the light under the door?

The rogue jolted at the sight of him, and Roric shoved his stake forward, but the rogue had better reflexes than some. He threw his arm up, knocking Roric's hand away and blocking the stake. It fell from Roric's hand and clattered to the ground. Before Roric could regain his balance, the rogue lunged for him, trying to knock him down.

Roric stumbled backwards down the hall, thumping into the walls, his hands scrambling at his holster for a weapon. Someone was bound to hear them and come to investigate! He wasn't sure it mattered, though. The bomb would go off before the rogues had a chance to react to

POSSESSED BY THE VAMPIRE

finding Roric.

But every moment he wasted fighting this vampire meant less time to save Caroline.   He felt the timer counting down with each beat of his heart. Overcome with fury, when his hand landed on the cool metal of his pistol, he yanked it out and shoved it into the rogue's chest.

The rogue's eyes widened at the feel of the metal pressed against his heart. He loosened his grip and took a step backwards, but Roric pulled the trigger, anyway. The gunshot boomed in the small hallway, echoing off the hardwood floors and doors and clouding the air with the burning scent of gunpowder.   The rogue staggered backwards, clutching his bleeding chest.

Surprised voices rose up for the other part of the house, but Roric wrenched open the basement door and leapt down the stairs before anyone had a chance to investigate. His feet slammed into the cement floor at the bottom, sending a bolt of pain up his legs, and his eyes quickly scanned the large, empty, cinderblock space. But all he saw was some dusty, cardboard boxes and a door at the other end of the basement.

He hurtled towards it, his muscular legs stretching, his feet barely touching the ground as he leapt across the distance separating him from the room where Caroline had to be. Then he skidded to a stop in front of it. He grabbed the doorknob and was surprised when it turned without resisting. He yanked the door open and was just about to step inside when the bomb went off.

It shook the whole house with a massive boom that vibrated through his body and immediately deafened him. Then the room in front of him disappeared as the room above collapsed on top of it in a clatter.   The drywall

168

ceiling crumbled in a cloud of dust that filled the air. The wooden joists in the floor above cracked and splintered and fell down like massive, jagged stakes, plunging into the pile of rubble. Roric jerked back, grabbing his heart as they pierced through, imagining them impaling Caroline's body.

"Caroline!"

When the shaking settled, he threw himself at the pile, grabbing chunks of wood and flinging them out of the room, desperate to find Caroline's body. Protruding nails raked at his skin, tearing long gouges in his flesh. The cloud of drywall dust mixed with the blood, caking his wounds in a thick, bloody paste. It filled his lungs, too, choking him. He coughed and sputtered and wiped at his grit-filled eyes with dirty hands.

None of that mattered. His body would heal, and so would hers. He just had to find her.

He didn't worry about what was going on upstairs. He gave no thought to how many rogues had been killed or how many had survived. He didn't care if his agents needed him to take down any that had escaped. His focus was singular.

He worked like a machine — grabbing a piece of debris with one hand and hurling it out of the room as he reached for another with the other hand, over and over again till his arms seized with cramps, the muscles tightening into thick ropes that pulsed under his flesh. Still, he ignored them, forcing his body to obey his commands.

He kept going, even after the pile was reduced enough that he could see the floor beneath it. Even when it was obvious that Caroline wasn't under it. When the last chunk of wood was removed, he stared at the bloody mattress in the corner of the room. He recognized it from the video call. That was where Caroline's body had lain, riddled with bullet holes. But she wasn't there now.

But that meant she was probably upstairs when the blast went off. Which meant her odds of survival were even less than when he thought she was buried under a pile of rubble.

He swallowed down the chalky lump in his throat and turned around, scrambling over the debris he'd hurled out into the other part of the basement. The rickety, wooden staircase had broken apart in places, but he jumped up it, anyway, holding tight to the railing in case the stairs collapsed under him.

CHAPTER NINETEEN

Caroline debated for only a few moments before making up her mind. Staying there, where Michael was sure to kill her, to avoid the risk of being caught before Serena could get to Roric might be noble, but she was too determined to survive to lie down and wait for death, or even rescue. She had to try.

She tottered over to the door to her prison on shaky legs, her makeshift stake clutched in her hand. When the knob turned and the door cracked open, she peeked through the crack. She couldn't see the entire basement, but it appeared to be empty. Feeling confident, she pushed the door open and stepped out. When no one whacked her upside the head or put a bullet in her, she breathed out a sigh of relief. But there were an unknown number of threats still between her and freedom.

She tiptoed up the stairs quickly, her tight muscles softening with each flex and her body strengthening. She still felt a little achy and sluggish, but if she was a human, she'd be dead, so she was incredibly grateful for her vampire healing abilities. Now if she could just sneak out without getting a stake in the heart or a bullet in the head. Serena had told her that there were guards at the door, so her only hope was that she could hide till something distracted them.

She cracked open the door at the top of the stairs and peeked into the hallway. She saw a figure dart into a room, but the rest of the hall was clear. The light came on in the room, so she figured the person would be in there for a moment.

She didn't have the luxury of time to be patient, so she took the opportunity and dashed out into the hallway. The front door was down the hall to her left, but the living room was that way, as well, and she was certain people would be in there. Plus, there might be other rogues out in front of the house, just arriving.

Her best bet was to go the other way and look for the back door, even though that meant passing the room she'd just seen someone go into. She hadn't been that way before, either, so she didn't know where she was going. She'd have to search for the door, which increased the likelihood of running into someone.

Not everyone knew who Roric's girlfriend was or what she looked like, so she might have been able to pass herself off as one of the rogues if anyone saw her, except that her clothes were bloody and riddled with bullet holes. That was kind of a giveaway. And the guards would certainly recognize her. Michael would have made sure of that.

But she could hear Michael talking from the other side of the house, which meant the meeting had started. Hopefully, most of the rogues would be in the meeting and not wandering around. She didn't know why one of them had just entered the room next to her, but he probably wouldn't stay there for long.

Adrenaline coursed through her veins, spurring her into action. With only a moment's hesitation, she turned towards her right and slipped down the hallway, he stocking feet gliding quietly on the hardwood floors. When she got to the end of the hall, she pressed her body up against the wall for a moment then stuck her head out to look into the room beyond.

It was a kitchen, and thankfully no one was in it because they would've seen her immediately. Her heart thundered in her chest, and her hands trembled at her sides as her breath rattled in and out in shaky gasps.

There was an exterior door with a small, blind-covered window against the back wall. Caroline padded over to it and stuck a finger in the blinds, spreading them just enough that she could peek out of them. Her belly clenched, expecting the face of a guard to be staring back at her, but she didn't see anyone out there.

There had to be one, though. Didn't there? Serena said their were guards, and Michael wasn't one to take too many chances. The guard was probably off to the side where she couldn't see him. She was lucky there wasn't a guard on the inside, too. She tightened her grip on her stake, wishing her palm wasn't damp and shaky.

The back stoop was dark, and so was the night beyond that. She didn't see anyone else out there, but there was a large expanse of grass that she'd have to cross, and she'd be totally exposed while she did so. But it was bordered by a small woods that she could easily hide in.

She had no idea where she was, but it didn't matter. Dawn was still hours away, so she had time to find her way home before the sun became a threat. A lump lodged in her throat as she thought about seeing Roric again. She was desperate to feel his arms around her. When a tear dripped onto her cheek, she wiped it away quickly and forced herself to get moving. Hesitating only increased her chances of being seen.

Suddenly, thumping noises behind her startled her. She threw a hand to her chest. Someone was in the hallway! Then a gunshot boomed, loud as a cannon in the small space.

She grabbed her belly as it clenched, assuming that someone had seen her and shot at her, but there was no exit wound and no pain. Who were they shooting at if it wasn't her? She was standing still; they wouldn't have missed if they'd been aiming for her.

Too afraid to look back, she yanked open the door and rushed outside, her stake held out in front of her, ready to plunge into the guard as soon as he saw her.

But the stoop was empty. The whole yard was. She quickly shut the door behind her before whoever was firing the gun saw her.

She pressed her back against the wood-sided wall behind the door and took a moment to catch her breath. She'd done it! She'd made it outside without anyone seeing her! It was a miracle, that was for sure. It was like someone had cleared the way for her. It didn't make any sense, but she didn't care to question it. All that mattered was that she was almost free.

All she had to do was cross the lawn. Since there was no one in sight, it should be easy. She let a smile curl her lips as her heart rate and breathing started to settle. The crickets chirped out a welcoming song, soothing her, and the fresh air reinvigorated her even though it was muggy.

But then an ear-piercing boom shattered the silence, and the house shook behind her, knocking her off balance, hurling her off the stoop and into the grass.   Startled, Caroline yelped and stumbled out into the yard then started running as fast as she could away from the house. The dark woods loomed closer, beckoning her.   She was almost there!

She was steps away from their cover when a spark flared in the woods and a pressure slammed into her.   It knocked her backwards at the same time the sound of a gunshot rang out.   Two more hits slammed into her body, and she fell to the ground with a thud.   Footsteps pounded towards her.

A voice called out, "Shoot 'em in the head so they can't get up!"

Suddenly, another bullet blasted into her skull, and the world around her started spinning as the bullet ricocheted through her brain.   Her senses short-circuited.   Her vision blurred then darkened, her ears echoed with a jumble of chaotic sounds.   Then she fell into an abyss of nothingness.

CHAPTER TWENTY

The house looked even worse than Roric imagined it would, but he forced himself to walk through it. He wouldn't give up till he'd combed every inch of it, looking for Caroline.

The rooms farther away from the blast sustained the least damage, but every window was shattered, furniture was knocked over, and some of the non-load bearing walls had buckled. Roric quickly searched every nook and cranny of every room, even though he'd looked in most of them before, tossing furniture out of the way and looking under beds and in closets in case she was hiding. He called out her name as he went, his voice sounding pained and desperate.

As he moved closer to where the bomb had been, a layer of ash coated everything. It gave him a sick sense of satisfaction knowing that dozens of rogues had been obliterated in one fell swoop, and hopefully anyone who escaped the blast had been gunned down by his agents when they stepped outside. But he couldn't help but wonder if some of that ash used to be Caroline. He couldn't let himself consider it, not till he'd exhausted all other possibilities.

He recognized ground zero as soon as he saw it. The walls were blown out, and there was a gaping hole in the floor, everything else around it charred and blackened. A few twisted fragments of metal were all that was left of some folding chairs. Otherwise, everything else was destroyed.

The ash was thick there, coating everything and floating in the air, the acrid dust creating a gray cloud that filled his nose, mouth, and lungs with every breath. He choked and gagged on it then blocked off his airflow, disgusted by the thought of inhaling the remains of so many vampires.

He carefully stepped to the hole and peered over the edge, looking down at the space below. Just as he suspected, the basement prison was directly beneath him. Thank God she hadn't been there when the blast went off. But where was she?

Roric went back to the basement door and tried to put himself in Caroline's shoes. If she'd tried to escape, where would she have gone? The front door was one direction, the back door was the other way. She would've known better that to go out the front door. She knew about the meeting and would've expected there to be vampires arriving for it. So she must've gone out the back way.

He tromped back towards the kitchen and the door he and Taven had entered. They'd taken out the guard on their way in. Had that allowed her to escape? But no, he would've seen her, wouldn't he? Unless she'd snuck past while he was in one of the bedrooms. He barked out a hollow laugh at the irony of the thought. But then his laugh caught in his throat and died when he realized that was the only possibility that gave her a chance at surviving.

The door hung open, left that way by the vampires who'd managed to survive the blast. Roric stood at the door for a moment and stared out at the lawn. He could see bodies littering the grass, and his agents were milling around.

"Roric!" Taven bellowed his name and hurtled towards him. He slammed into him like a freight train, wrapping his arms around him tight enough to cut off his circulation. Roric stumbled backwards but held onto Taven for support.

Eventually, Taven loosened his grip and pulled away enough that he could look at him. "You're alive! I thought you bit it, you asshole! Where have you been all this time?"

"I found the place where they were keeping Caroline, but the blast zone was right on top of her. I was digging through the rubble, looking for her, but I couldn't find her."

Taven's face crumpled till it looked the way Roric's felt. "Shit, man. I'm so sorry."

He pulled Roric tight again, hugging him. Hot tears welled up in Roric's eyes as he let the truth sink in. Caroline hadn't escaped. If she had, she'd be out here with Taven. Caroline was gone.

He quivered at first then started shaking violently as sobs wracked his body. Taven held onto him as he collapsed against him. He heard a keening sound and thought it might be him, but he couldn't tell. He was too lost in his grief.

He eventually dropped to the ground when his knees buckled beneath him. He wrapped his arms around them and hugged them to his body as if he was holding Caroline. Taven sat down beside him for a while, but there was nothing he could do to comfort him.

One of the other agents approached with a question, but Roric couldn't understand it. The voice was like Charlie Brown's teacher, the words meaningless sounds. Taven answered him, and the agent nodded and walked off. Eventually, all the agents headed out, except for Taven, leaving the lawn empty except for the bodies strewn around the grass.

A long while later, Taven tapped him on the shoulder. "Roric, you ready to go home? The sun's coming up soon."

Roric lifted his head and stared at the lightening horizon. The sun was rising, but his world was still cloaked in darkness. It might be that way forever.

"I'm just gonna stay here," he said, keeping his eyes on the sunrise. He was done. He'd accomplished his mission. Michael and most of the rogues were dead. There was nothing left for him to do. He might as well end his misery.

"No way, bro. I'm not gonna let you do that. I'll drag your sorry ass to the car if I have to, but you're not committing suicide out here."

"Why not? What have I got to live for?"

"I need you, and so does Dad. Come on, you can hide out in your room for the rest of eternity if you want, but I'm not gonna leave you out here to do something stupid." Taven grabbed his arm and jerked him up, practically pulling it out of the socket.

Roric growled and snapped his teeth at him, but he didn't have the energy to fight him. He let his brother drag him back the same way they'd approached the farmhouse. They'd only gone a few yards before something caught his eye. Blonde hair splayed out in the grass, coated in blood. It reminded him of Caroline's the first night he'd found her.

He couldn't resist. He yanked his arm away from Taven and rushed over to the body. Black leggings covering long, shapely legs. A white tee shirt stained with dried blood and riddled with bullet holes. Blood coating her face and staining her hair dark red. A scent he would recognize anywhere. Her head was facing away from him, so he knelt down and turned it towards him.

Caroline.

A painful gasp tore from his throat as he reached for her, lifting her head up. Her eyes were closed, her mouth slack, no breath escaping. She'd been shot in the forehead. But bullet wounds weren't fatal to vampires, not even head wounds. She might not come back exactly the same, but she would come back to him. Tremors shook through his body as relief washed over him. He hadn't lost her.

"Holy shit." Taven hovered over them, gawking at her.

Roric slid his hands under her and lifted her up, cradling her limp body in his arms. Her arms and legs flapped lifelessly, and her head lolled over his elbow. Roric stared at her, emotions swirling inside of him, too many for him to process. They made him dizzy. He forced his body to stiffen so he wouldn't drop her.

"Go get the car, Taven," he croaked out, not taking his eyes off her.

Taven hustled off. Roric stayed there, holding her and whispering assurances to her or himself, he wasn't sure which, till Taven pulled up beside him in his cruiser.

Taven jumped out and opened the back door, and Roric carefully laid Caroline down in the back seat. Then he climbed into the passenger seat. "Let's go home now."

Taven nodded and peeled out of there. They were home before the sun broke the horizon. Roric carried Caroline up to his suite and laid her on the bed. Taven followed him in.

"Hey, I'm gonna go see Ivy, but you call me if you need me, okay?"

Roric nodded and waved him away. There was nothing Taven could do for him. All they could do was wait for Caroline's body to heal itself.

When Taven left, closing the door behind him, Roric tore himself away from Caroline just long enough to run the water in the bathtub. He fiddled with the water temperature till it was just right. Then he came back and stripped her filthy, bloody clothes off, throwing them in the trash can.

He lifted her up and carried her to the bathroom then laid her down in the wide tub. The dried blood that coated her body began to wash away, turning the water pink. Roric took a washcloth and scrubbed away the rest of it, revealing flawless skin. She looked perfect. He could only pray her mind would recover as well as her body. Would she come back as the Caroline he loved, or someone different? He knew he would love her, anyway.

The only remaining wound was the hole in her forehead, but even it was almost closed. Had the bullet been expelled yet? He didn't know. If it hadn't, she'd go through more torture when it did. Selfishly, he hoped he didn't have to watch that. But he wasn't leaving her side till she woke up again.

When her body was clean, he carefully lowered her head into the water and scrubbed the blood out of her hair, shampooing it several times till the locks looked blonde again. By then, the water was red and cloudy, so he pulled the plug and let it drain. Then he turned on the shower and let it rinse her.

His own body was sopping wet and covered in ash and dust and blood, so he stripped off his clothes and stepped in with her, keeping his eyes on her as he scrubbed his body clean. It was kind of macabre, having her lifeless body in the shower with him, but he wasn't about to leave her. When she woke up, and she would wake up, he didn't want her to be alone and frightened.

When he was done, he shut off the water, dried himself, then dried Caroline, wrapping her soaking wet hair in a towel. He carried her back to the bed and dressed her in soft, cotton lounge pants and one of his tee shirts. Then he put on some boxers and climbed in bed with her. He pulled her body into his and wrapped his arm around her, snuggling her head against his chest. She was warm, and her heart was beating. That was enough for now.

He cried out when he felt her warm breath rush against him. She was breathing again! Vampires didn't need to breathe to survive like humans, but they did it instinctively, anyway. It helped them blend into society, for one thing, and heightened their sense of smell. Plus, Roric thought it made him feel more alive when he was breathing. He took Caroline's breath as another sign that she was recovering, even though she still looked lifeless.

A few hours later, her fingers started to curl into him, and her mouth moved a little as a tiny moan escaped. Roric's heart started racing. He sat up and shook her shoulder. "Caroline? Are you awake?"

She didn't answer him, but she burrowed against him like she was looking for something. Maybe she needed to drink. He rolled her over onto her back and propped her up some with the pillows. Then he tore open his wrist and held it to her mouth.

The blood coated her lips at first, but Roric stuck a finger between them and opened her mouth up. Once the blood started pouring down her throat, her body responded. Her mouth started moving, and her lips suctioned against his skin. Her throat bobbed as she swallowed.

A few minutes later, Roric pulled his arm away, but her hands reached up and grabbed him, pressing his wrist to her mouth again. Roric scrunched his face against the onslaught of emotions threatening to overtake him. She was moving! She held his arm to her mouth for several more minutes before finally letting her hands drop.

Suddenly, her body seized, and she screamed, an ear-shattering, gut-wrenching sound that tore through his body like a bandsaw, slicing him apart. Her eyes widened, and her mouth gaped as her chest rose off the bed like it was being pulled by a rope then collapsed again.

Roric jumped up onto his knees and hovered over her, his hands roving uselessly over her body. "Caroline, what's wrong? What's the matter?"

Sweat broke out all over her body, coating her skin with a sickly sheen. She flailed her arms and legs as her head whipped back and forth, agony twisting her features. Her mouth opened and closed in a soundless scream. When she squeezed her eyes closed and pinched her brow, a small bump bulged from her forehead.

She screamed once more, the sound reverberating off

the walls, so loud the whole neighborhood could probably hear it. Then her whole body clenched up, her limbs twisting like gnarled tree branches and her hands turning into claws.

Finally, the skin on her forehead split open, and a chunk of silver spit out of the wound and tumbled down onto the pillow, leaving a bloody trail.

Caroline's face and body relaxed. Her limbs flopped lifelessly to her side, and her mouth hung open. She laid there, unmoving, for several long seconds.

Panic ignited Roric's body. He leapt up, his body trembling wildly, and shook her. "No, no, no! You're not dead! Come back, Caroline! Come back!"

He stumbled backwards and fell to the ground when her eyes opened again, the peridot gemstones blinding him with their brightness, searching his. "Roric?"

He gasped, and his own eyes filled with tears. "Caroline!"

She lifted herself up with her elbows and looked down at him. "Are you okay?"

He chuckled, but then he couldn't stop. His body shook with laughter, and tears dripped down his cheeks as the anxiety poured out of him. Caroline stared at him with concern as he tried to get ahold of himself. Finally, he managed to pull himself back up to the bed. He stroked her hair, her cheek, her lips, his hands shaking. She was back!

"Am I okay? No, I'm not okay. I'm losing my shit here. Are you okay?"

She flexed her body like she was looking for injuries. "Yeah, I guess so. I feel kind of sore, and my head hurts. What happened?"

He curled up next to her and pulled her into his arms,

185

smoothing his hand down her hair over and over again. "What do you remember?"

She pinched her brow and pursed her lips as she thought. "I got out of the house. There was a loud noise, then something hit me."

"You escaped, then the bomb went off, then one of the agents shot you down, thinking you were a rogue. God, I'm so sorry." He pulled her closer and pressed his lips to her forehead, trying to kiss away the worry wrinkles.

She pulled away and looked up at him, her brow still creased. "Why don't I remember?"

Roric winced, wishing she'd let it drop. It was a blessing that she didn't remember. But Caroline was too stubborn for that. She'd pester him till he told her. He sighed and rubbed her forehead smooth with his finger. "You got shot in the head. You've been comatose all day. But you just ejected the bullet."

Her eyes widened and her mouth fell open. She scrambled out of his arms. "I was braindead? What if I'm not… normal anymore?"

He stroked a hand down her arm then clasped his hand over hers. "Do you remember me? Do you remember that I love you and you agreed to mate with me?"

She frowned, but then her lips curled up in a soft smile. "Of course."

"Then you're fine, baby. Right as rain. That's all you need to remember." He pulled her down then and pressed her body to the mattress as he lowered himself on top of her. He probably ought to give her a little more time to recover, but she seemed okay to him, and he couldn't resist proving to himself that she was alive and well and still belonged to him.

CHAPTER TWENTY-ONE

Taven hustled away from Roric's room and down the hall to his own. Seeing Caroline's battered, lifeless body had his nerves twisted up in tangled knots and made him anxious to find Ivy. He grabbed the doorknob and shoved the door open, his chest heaving and his breath blowing hard and loud through his nostrils.

Ivy sat on his black leather couch, looking like she belonged there, watching a rerun of The Vampire Diaries. She swiveled her head around to look at him then scrambled to pull herself off the sofa. "Taven!"

She rushed towards him, and he closed the distance in two long strides then wrapped his thick arms around her trim body and pressed her to him till every inch of her was touching him. If she was still human, he would've hurt her, he was holding her so tightly, but her vampire body was strong enough to take it. She hugged him back, winding her thin arms around his middle, digging her nails in. She buried her face in his tee shirt, and her hot breath stoked a fire in him.

He wanted to toss her onto the bed and have his way

with her, but he couldn't do that. Not till they had a conversation. They had things to work out if this relationship was going to last, and he wouldn't take her again till he knew she belonged to him.

He hugged her tight for another moment, savoring the feel of her in case it was his last chance. Her tiny waist, her lush breasts pressed against him, her long, silky hair, the intoxicating, spicy scent of her. Focusing on her attributes only made him more desperate for her. He had to make this work between them.

Eventually, he relaxed his arms and let go of her. She seemed reluctant to pull away, and it gave him hope that she felt the same way that he did. He didn't know what she saw in him — he was a loud, pushy asshole most of the time with commitment issues and a jealous streak. He knew that. He'd have to work on it. But for some reason she was still interested in him.

"How did it go? You were gone for so long. I thought... I thought something bad had happened." Her question threw him. Then he felt like a jerk.

He'd forgotten that she was waiting around to hear from him. He'd been so caught up in Roric's situation that he didn't stop to think that she was still worried about whether he'd made it out alive. He should've called her. He really was an asshole. But she'd stayed all this time, waiting for him. That meant a lot.

"It went good. Just like we wanted. I snuck in, planted the bomb, and got out of there before it went off. Roric couldn't find Caroline, though—"

She gasped and dug her fingernails into his chest as her face crumpled.

"No, no, it's okay. She made it out on her own before

the bomb went off, but an agent thought she was a rogue and shot her down. But we found her. She's... recovering." That was the best way he could think of to put it. He didn't know if she'd be okay, or not, but at least she wasn't blown to bits.

"Thank God." Ivy buried her face in his chest again, wiping her tears. He stroked her body, incredibly thankful that she was whole and well and hadn't had to endure any of the torture that Caroline had been through.

"Ivy, there's something I need to tell you."

She tensed up again and looked up with him with anxiety quivering in the deep, dark pools of her eyes.

"Let's go sit down." He took her hand and pulled her over to the couch then dropped down and rubbed his face with his hands. She sat down beside him and put her hand on his leg.

"A few years ago, I was dating a girl named Talia. We'd been going out for a while, and things had gotten serious. Or, at least, I thought they had. I asked her to mate with me."

Ivy clenched up and pulled her hand back into her own lap. Taven reached for it and slid his fingers through hers. "She turned me down and broke up with me. She'd been seeing some other guy behind my back. She ended up mating with him."

Ivy's mouth fell open, and her eyes misted over with sympathy. "I'm sorry, Taven. That must've hurt. Do you..." She dropped her eyes to her lap. "Do you still have feelings for her?"

He shoved a hand through his messy hair and snarled. "God, no. I got over her real quick when I found out she'd been cheating on me. But I'm telling you this because I want you to understand where I'm coming from. I don't trust easily, and I'm a jealous bastard. Anytime I see you around another guy, I go ballistic, thinking you're doing the same thing she did."

She rubbed the inseam of her tight jeans. "I'm sorry. I haven't helped things. Every person I've ever cared about has left me, so I have a hard time believing that you're going to stick around. It seems like you push me away whenever I take a step closer."

"I've pushed you away because I was scared that if I got too serious, you'd leave me and I'd be torn apart. I know I'm not exactly great boyfriend material. There are plenty of better guys out there you could be with. I keep waiting for you to realize that and dump me for one of them."

"Why do you think that, Taven? Just because Talia dumped you? She was an idiot. You're strong, and smart, and passionate, and gorgeous." Her lips curled up in a smile at that, and she stroked a finger down his face.

"I'm Damon."

"What?" She wrinkled her brow and shook her head in confusion.

He waved his hand towards the TV where Ian Somerhalder was flashing his sexy, blue eyes and doing something terrible to somebody. "Damon. On the show. I'm a ruthless, dangerous, out of control monster."

Ivy laughed at that. It made her face soften and her dark eyes sparkle. "You're not Damon. But so what if you are? He's everybody's favorite character. And Elena loves him, just the way he is."

He grinned at her, his heart suddenly ten times lighter. He didn't realize how heavy it had gotten. "Am I as sexy as Damon?"

She rolled her eyes at him, giggling. "You know you are. Why do you even ask that?"

He had a lot of comebacks for that, but he didn't want to joke around anymore. He turned to face her head on and looked straight at her so she'd know he was serious. "We have something special, Ivy, and I don't want to lose you. I love you. If I get serious about this, you have to, too. No other guys. I can't handle that."

She put her hands on his arms, wrapping her fingers around his biceps, and shook her head. "You're the only guy I want, Taven. But you have to promise never to leave me."

He smirked. "Sounds like we're making vows."

She gulped and nodded, and the smirk fell off his face. She really wanted to commit to him. She was just waiting for him to want it, too.

He pulled her hands off his arms and twined his fingers with hers. "Will you mate with me, Ivy? Will you promise to be mine forever?"

Her face split in a brilliant, glorious smile, her bright white teeth shining against her honey gold skin. "I thought you'd never ask. Of course I will."

He grabbed her by the back of the head and brought her lips to his then kissed her fervently, his lips claiming her. She tasted as good as she looked — sweet as honey, spicy as cinnamon. He savored her, reveling in the fact that she was his and he could taste her whenever he wanted to.

She ran her hands up his chest, swirling her fingers around his nipples, then over his shoulders, her fingers digging into the thick muscle. Then she rose up onto her knees, sliding her hands down his back.

He grabbed her waist and pulled her closer then stroked his hands up and down her back. His fingers slid under her loose, black tank to find her silky skin. She shivered under his touch.

She moved her legs to either side of his hips then dropped her crotch down onto his, pressing against his erection, taunting him. She ground herself against him, and his breath grew ragged, desperate.

He couldn't stand it anymore, he had to bury himself in her. He picked her up and lifted them off the couch. She wrapped her legs around his waist, keeping their centers aligned, and kept kissing him as he carried her over to the bed.

He dropped them down onto to the bed, landing on top of her. She grunted but didn't complain. His erection throbbed with the added pressure.

He didn't want to pull himself away from her, but there were way too many clothes between them. He needed to feel her hot skin sliding against his. He shimmied off of her and stood up then tore his clothes off. She grinned at him and wiggled out of her clothes while she watched him. In moments, they were both naked.

She was so beautiful. Naturally tan skin that glowed against his black silk duvet, a trim figure but with round curves in all the right places, full breasts, dark pink nipples that begged to be sucked.

She lifted herself up onto her elbows then scooted back till she was in the middle of the bed, presenting herself like a piece of gold jewelry on a velvet tray. It made him hesitate for a moment. "Ivy, maybe we shouldn't do this yet."

Her face puckered with rejection and anger. "What the

hell, Taven? You've got to be kidding!"

"No, no, I mean, I just thought maybe you'd like to have a mating ceremony first, you know? Make it official."

"You mean like a wedding?"

"Yeah, kind of like that. A vampire wedding." His mind conjured up an image of her in a mating robe, and he was shocked at how badly he wanted to see it for real.

Surprisingly, she cringed. Didn't every woman fantasize about a big wedding? "Would we have to... mate... in front of other people?" She glanced at his penis, bobbing eagerly.

He chuckled and kneeled on the end of the bed. "No, it's just a commitment ceremony. The actual mating comes after."

She got a relieved look on her face that turned thoughtful. "Oh. Who would we invite? I don't really have any family."

"Well, my family is kind of well-known in the vampire community. Pretty much every vampire in town would want to come to it."

She winced again. "That's a lot of attention."

Ivy was never one to shy away from attention. There had to be something else she was worried about. Did she think people wouldn't approve of her? There might be some talk, but he didn't care what anyone else thought. He was proud to mate with her.

"We don't have to have a ceremony if you don't want to. All that matters to me is what comes after. But I'm pretty sure Roric and Caroline are going to have a huge ass ceremony, and I don't want you to feel like you missed out. But whatever you want is fine with me. We can even have a joint ceremony, if you want. Roric suggested that earlier."

She perked up at that. "He did? So, you were talking to him about mating me?"

"Well, yeah. We talk sometimes." Not really, but they should. The few personal conversations they'd had lately had been kind of nice.

"That might be good. Caroline doesn't have any family, either."

"So, do you want to wait and talk to them about a joint ceremony?"

"Yeah, maybe. But can we still have sex?" She sat up and reached for his deflating penis. It jerked to life again as soon as her hand wrapped around it.

"Caroline won't be in any condition to talk for hours. Days, even." He climbed on top of her, pushing her back onto the bed, and settled between her legs. The rogues were dead, his loved ones were safe, and he had nothing better to do than lose himself in Ivy. He grabbed a condom and slipped it on. They'd talk about a family later. Then he buried himself inside her.

CHAPTER TWENTY-TWO

Piper stared nervously at the embossed gold lettering on the heavy, linen invitation. Then she picked up the phone and tapped on her favorites list. Her finger hovered over Davede's name. It was no big deal. She should call him. He'd probably be happy to go with her.

But still she hesitated. Were they serious enough to go to a wedding together? Well, not exactly a wedding. A mating ceremony. But, whatever. It was a ceremony to celebrate a lifetime commitment made between two people... er, vampires. And that was something you went to with someone you were serious about, not just whatever guy you were dating at the moment. It was too intimate, otherwise.

But what if he got the wrong idea? What if he thought that meant she was ready to get mated? Which she most certainly was not, even though she wanted to spend practically every spare moment with him lately. That didn't mean she was ready to commit the rest of her life to him. No, better not put herself in an awkward situation.

She put the phone down and walked away. She could

go stag. It would be fun. She might even meet someone interesting. Dance the night away with a bunch of hot, single vampires. But her heart pinched at the thought of that. She'd couldn't do that. She'd feel like she was betraying Davede.

What if Davede was there? He wasn't close friends with any of the wedding party, but the vampire community was tight knit. He had probably gotten an invitation. Had he thought about asking her to go with him?

What if he had, and he'd decided against it? The thought made her scowl. How dare he not invite her to be his date? She was his girlfriend! He said he was serious about her. So why wouldn't he ask her to the ceremony? She'd just about worked herself into a tizzy when the phone rang.

She yanked it off the table. Davede's name was on the screen. She jabbed at the green button, snarling. "Hello?"

"Uh, hey. Are you okay? You sound upset, or something."

She sighed and pushed down her irritation. She was being stupid. She'd already decided she wasn't going to ask Davede to go to the wedding with her, so why was she irritated that he hadn't asked her?

She forced herself to sound cheerful. "I'm fine. It's nothing."

"Okay, well, I don't know how you'll feel about this, but I got an invitation to Roric and Taven's mating ceremony, and I was wondering if you'd like to go with me."

A smile curled up the edges of Piper's lips, and she bit down on a finger to keep from squealing.

Davede took her silence for reticence and quickly

backpedaled. "It's okay if you don't want to. I just thought you probably got an invitation too and maybe you'd like to go together."

"I'd like that a lot," she blurted out.

Davede breathed out a shaky sigh into the phone. "Great. Should I pick you up at 9 next Saturday, then?"

"Yeah, that sounds perfect." Her mind instantly switched over to her other worry. "Uh, Davede? What do girls wear to mating ceremonies? I've never been to one. Is it like a human wedding?"

He chuckled at her. "I've never been to one of those, so I can't tell you. But just wear a nice dress and you'll be fine. I like that black one of yours." His voice got a little husky like he was thinking about how she looked in it.

Two weeks later, Piper zipped herself into a new, green silk dress. Davede had meant well, but everyone knows you don't wear black to a wedding. Of course, vampires really liked black, so maybe it would've been okay. But still, she appreciated the chance to buy something new.

Since Roric and Taven were rich and prestigious, she assumed their mating ceremony was going to be extravagant. The dress she'd picked was long and elegant with a high slit up the slim skirt and decorative ruching on the vee neck bodice. She thought it made her look tall, trim, and fabulous.

She'd twisted her hair up into a chignon and done up her face with dramatic, nighttime makeup. She felt like a movie star about to walk the red carpet. She just hoped she didn't stumble around like a drunk in her four-inch heels. She was used to wearing flats every day.

Customarily early, Davede rang the doorbell a few

minutes before 9. Piper gawked when she opened it and saw him standing there in a custom-tailored, black suit with a stiff, white dress shirt with French cuffs and a black bowtie. She never thought a bowtie could look so sexy. But with his hair freshly cut and styled and his shoes shined to a mirror polish, Davede was going to give the grooms a run for their money.

He stared at her while she stared at him. "Wow, you look amazing," they both said in unison.

Piper chuckled and leaned in to kiss him. With her heels on, they were almost the same height. He wrapped his arms around her and pulled her closer. She liked the way they fit together. She might have to wear those heels more often.

When they pulled apart, he held out his arm to escort her to the car. She took it, grateful for the steady support. She was kind of wobbly.

"So, do you know where you're going? Cuz they forgot to put the address on the invitation." Piper double checked the invitation as soon as Davede started driving. Nope, nothing there but the date, time, and names of the honorees.

Davede smiled and glanced at her. "They didn't forget. All the mating ceremonies take place in the lair."

"The lair? What is that, like the Bat Cave? Is that where all the evil vampires plot their attacks?" Piper gawked at him, picturing the old Dracula movies.

Davede chuckled. "Back centuries ago when vampires first settled in the area, before humans knew about vampires, they didn't try to blend in with society. Instead, they lived in a series of caves out in the desert."

Piper grimaced. A cave? She was wearing a tight

gown and four-inch heels! She was supposed to hike into a cave? She hoped they'd modernized it. Put in paved walkways, or something. If not, Davede was going to have to carry her. She grinned. That might be kind of fun, though. She could work with the whole damsel in distress act. Davede was still talking, so she forced herself out of her daydreams and back to what he was saying.

"They came and went only at night, and no one knew they were there. They lived that way for a long time, but when the vampire population got big enough that they needed more space, some moved out and assimilated into human society. Eventually, almost everyone left."

"Almost everyone? You mean there are still vampires living there?" Piper squirmed, imagining vampires turning into bats and flying out of caves.

"Yeah, some of the oldest ones never had any desire to leave. I think there are half a dozen or so originals still left."

"Originals? Like Klaus on The Vampire Diaries?"

Davede outright laughed at her. She supposed she deserved that. Her knowledge of vampires was based on TV shows and movies. She knew they weren't very accurate, but some of it was true. But she didn't know how to separate fact from fiction. If her stupid brother was willing to talk to her about it, he could probably tell her everything there was to know, but no, he refused to discuss anything about vampires with her. Said it gave her too many ideas.

"I mean the ones who first came to Modesa."

"Hundreds of years ago."

"Yeah."

Whoa. She knew vampires lived a long time, but it

was hard to imagine that some of them had been alive for centuries. She couldn't help it. Her curiosity was insatiable. "So, what do they look like? Can you tell that they're hundreds of years old?"

Davede shrugged. "I don't think so, but then, I'm used to what they look like. It will be interesting to hear your take on things. There haven't been very many humans who've been to the lair."

Piper shivered. "And came out alive, you mean."

Davede frowned and shook his head then turned down the air conditioner. "Most vampires feed off each other, remember? It's only been the last ten years or so that feeding from humans has become more normal. The old vampires have never tasted a human, never been to the blood clinic or drank from a blood bag. Feeding is intimately tied to relationships for them."

Piper kind of liked the idea of that. Sort of like how humans used to reserve sex for marriage. It made it seem more special. Davede was a modern vampire, raised in a world where feeding was just as casual as sex, but the tone of his voice made him sound nostalgic. "Do you ever wish things were like they used to be?"

He looked at her, his eyes glinting with complicated emotions. "If they were, I never would've gone out with you."

Piper swallowed back her own emotions. Davede was a traditionalist at heart, but he'd given up a lot of his dreams to be with her. She felt unworthy of his devotion. Could she give him what he wanted? When he looked at her like that, it was hard to remember why she was resisting. She thought she needed freedom to do whatever she wanted, but all she wanted to do was be with him.

What would she do if she was a vampire and they weren't together? Go out and drink from random vampires just for the thrill of it? Now that she'd experienced the pleasure of feeding someone she cared about, that had no appeal anymore.

She'd been so caught up in their conversation, she didn't notice where they were going till Davede pulled to a stop in a row full of cars lit only by moonlight. They were literally in the middle of the desert. Piper got out and stared at the huge, black sky dotted with stars. There was nothing but sand, rocks, and scrub for miles around.

Davede slid his arm through hers as she gaped at the scenery. The land was hard-packed and smooth, so she didn't have much trouble walking. He led her towards a large rock formation where an official-looking vampire checked their invitations, but she didn't see a cave entrance anywhere.

"This might be challenging for you in those shoes. Would you like me to carry you?"

Piper's lips curled up in a grin, and she nodded. She was getting her fantasy, after all. Davede scooped her up like she weighed nothing then jumped over a huge boulder, landing in a crevasse. Another boulder overhead blocked out the moonlight and draped the cave entrance in shadows, hiding it from casual observers. Piper gulped at the inky blackness. She knew vampires had good eyesight, but how could they see anything when there was no light at all?

Thankfully, Davede didn't set her down. She clung to him, shivering as he walked down into the black hole. The cave was quite a bit cooler than the warm night, with a dampness that left her chilled. Or maybe that was just her nerves. They twisted through the cave for a minute, then suddenly the space was aglow with yellow light. Oil lamps sat on ledges carved in the stone all around a large cavern. They flickered, casting shadows on the craggy walls. Between them hung ancient tapestries depicting scenes of wars, lovers, and blood-drinking.

On the back wall, hundreds of strange names were carved in the stone in long columns that stretched to the high ceiling where stalactites hung down, threatening to impale the hundred of vampires packed into the space. Piper supposed the threat of mortal injury didn't cross their minds like it did hers. Below each list of names, a large, intricately-carved, vase-shaped container, with gold decorations, sat on a ledge next to a matching chalice. Piper was pretty sure one of them was the Holy Grail that Indiana Jones had been looking for.

Davede set Piper down, but she clung to his arm, gawking at the horde of vampires and the symbolic decor. "Davede, I do not belong here! This is like, a sacred vampire synagogue, or something!"

"It kind of is, but you're fine. You got an invitation. They started letting select humans in here after vampires came out to the public. But you are one of very few who's had the privilege."

She kept her voice low and solemn even though the room was buzzing with voices. "I won't abuse it. I won't ever tell anyone about this place. It's too special."

Davede introduced her as his girlfriend to a few people whose names she promptly forgot. She thought they'd find it strange that he had a human girlfriend, but instead, most of them gave her a knowing look like they were in on some secret she didn't know about. Davede just smiled along with them. They probably assumed that she and Davede planned to get mated, and he was eating it up.

She frowned at that. That was exactly why she'd been hesitant to ask Davede to accompany her. But she was grateful he was with her. She'd feel totally out of place, otherwise. She didn't know anyone there except him and his parents. Well, and the wedding party, but they were probably down one of the tunnels that branched off from the main area, getting ready.

After milling around for fifteen minutes, Piper's toes felt like sardines squished in a can. "Is this where the ceremony will be held, or in another part of the cave?"

"In here."

"But there aren't any chairs. Do we have to stand for the whole thing?" She was really regretting her shoe choice.

"Don't worry." Davede grinned at her but didn't explain.

Moments later, a male vampire with long, black hair dressed in an ornate, red robe decorated with black and gold filigree stepped onto a platform and blew a brass horn. It gave a deep bellow that echoed loudly around the chamber. At once, everyone stopped talking and turned to face him, like soldiers, lining up in formation.

The men all dropped to one knee, keeping the other one bent in front of them like a seat. The women perched on the men's thighs, wrapping their arms around the men's necks. The young children stood next to their parents. Along the back wall, other vampires stood, as well. Were they the unmated?

Piper jumped and glanced down at Davede who had taken the same position as most of the other men. He gestured for her to sit on his leg. It was quiet enough she could hear her heart beating, so she didn't want to argue with him or ask any questions, but she had a feeling they were supposed to be standing in the back. She'd have words with him about that later.

The vampire on the platform put down the horn on a carved, wooden podium and addressed the crowd with a smooth, mellow voice that was somehow soft and booming at the same time. "Good evening to you, fellow brothers and sisters of the Modesa clan. It is a pleasure and an honor to officiate this sacred occasion."

"We are honored by your presence, Lord Artemis, son of Klaudius, son of Lehman," every voice said in unison, except Piper, of course, who couldn't squeak out a sound if she tried. She felt as out of place as she did that one time she went to a Catholic mass and didn't know when to sit or stand or what to say. Why hadn't she asked Davede more about what was going to happen tonight?

Hopefully, he wouldn't let her make a fool of herself. His breath blew warm and soft on her neck, and his hand curled around her waist, reassuring her. He had a content smile on his face. Piper tried to relax her own tense expression and enjoy the experience.

"We are here this evening to honor the union of not one but two couples. Let us welcome Roric Asheron, son of Kendar, son of Malik, son of Halcyon, and his intended, Caroline Weston." As he said the names of Roric's ancestors, the men stood up, their mates beside them.

The vampire turned towards one of the tunnels off to the side and stretched out a hand. Roric and Caroline appeared, arm in arm, and walked over to the platform then stepped up onto it and stood beside the officiant, facing the crowd. They both wore robes similar to the one that Lord

Artemis wore, but the decorations were different. Roric's was black with red embroidery down the center and along the bottom of the sleeves, and Caroline's was the opposite, red with black decorations. Her long, blonde hair was twisted up in a fancy updo.

"Let us also welcome Taven Asheron, son of Kendar, son of Malik, son of Halcyon, and his intended, Ivy Evans." Lord Artemis turned the other way, and Taven and Ivy came out the same way Roric and Caroline had, wearing the same type of robes.

Did they not name Caroline and Ivy's ancestors because they were dead, or because they weren't vampires? Piper added it to the list of questions she wanted to quiz Davede about as soon as they had a chance to talk again.

Lord Artemis held out both hands, and the couples stepped forward then turned towards each other and clasped their hands in between their chests. The guys both looked excited, but the girls looked nervous. Hopefully, the guys had gone over what to expect with them better than Davede had.

The officiant walked over to one of the ledges on the wall and picked up the chalice. Then he carried it over to Roric and Caroline. He stood behind them, holding the large, decorative cup between their hands. "Roric and Caroline, do you offer yourself to each other, that you may be joined for all eternity in blood, body, and soul?"

They let go of each other's hands and each held up a wrist to the other's mouth. Piper tensed. Were they going to drink from each other in front of everyone? Instead, they each bit into the other's wrist then pressed their arms together, holding them over the chalice. Their blood dripped down into the cup, mixing together.

Piper swallowed a hard lump in her throat. Those were some intense vows. She'd been told that vampires mated for life, there was no divorce or separation, other than death. It was hard to imagine making that kind of commitment to anything, even the person you loved. She couldn't stop herself from whispering her concerns to Davede. "How can they be so sure that they want to be bound together forever? What happens if they change their mind?"

Davede gave her a curious look and whispered back. "Mating is a decision, but staying mated isn't. Once they're mated, their bodies become like one. They won't have any desire to be separated."

The people beside them were looking at them, but Piper didn't care. She needed to understand this. "But what about Roric and Taven's parents? Caroline told me their mom committed suicide."

Davede shook his head. "She was mentally ill. She went out in the sun unprotected. No one knows if she really intended to commit suicide, or if she just wasn't thinking straight."

Piper grimaced. "So I don't have anything to worry about unless I go crazy."

Davede gave her a sly smile. "You have a lot of questions about mating for someone who doesn't want to get mated."

"A girl has the right to change her mind." Piper smirked at the look on Davede's face.

He squeezed her tight and nuzzled his mouth against her ear, sending tingles up and down her body. "Believe me, if you get mated, you won't want to change your mind."

Piper quieted down for the rest of the ceremony. After Caroline and Roric had bled into the cup for a while, the bleeding slowed till there was only the occasional drip. They pulled their wrists apart and held them to each other's mouth so the blood could be licked clean. Their wounds had already healed.

Lord Artemis held up the chalice. "With this blood, the two shall become one."

Then he handed it to Roric who took a sip before passing it to Caroline. She drank, too, then gave the cup back to Artemis. He carried it over to the ledge and set it down. Roric and Caroline followed him. Then he moved a tall ladder wide enough for two people in front of the column of names behind the chalice. It was only then that Piper realized all the surnames in that column were Asheron. Each column must represent a different family.

Roric picked up the chalice in one hand and took Caroline's hand with the other. Together, they climbed up the ladder till they got to the last set of names at the top. They belonged to Roric's parents. Roric took his index finger and pressed it against the wall of the cave then carved his own name, digging his finger into the stone with a screech. When he was done, Caroline wrote hers the same way, and Roric added his last name at the end. Then they each dipped their finger in the chalice and traced their engraved names with the blood till the letters were filled in with red.

After that, they climbed down the ladder and Roric handed the chalice back to Artemis. He lifted the lid on the large vase. "Your bonded blood joins that of your ancestors."

He poured the blood into the vase, then he and

everyone else chanted out, "May your line live on for all eternity!"

The response sent shivers down Piper's spine. This was the most intense ceremony she'd ever been to. The ceremony repeated for Taven and Ivy. Piper eagerly joined in when they said the final line. Then Lord Artemis put the chalice back on the ledge and moved to the front of the platform. "Let us honor this union with the blood of our ancestors."

Several male vampires walked up to the platform then. Each took down one of the vases, then they carried them towards the center of the platform where another, much larger chalice sat. The vampires encircled the chalice then simultaneously poured some of the blood from each vase into it.

Piper tensed up again. Were they seriously going to drink that? How old was that blood? Did vampire blood go bad? She hoped they didn't expect her to drink it!

Lord Artemis took the chalice and held it up. He and everyone else chanted, "May our line live on for all eternity!"

Then Artemis took a drink and passed it to the nearest vampire on the platform. Each of them took a sip. The last one handed it back to Artemis who finished it off. The crowd broke out in a cheer, and everyone started moving again. Piper stayed still for a long moment, taking it all in.

"Well, what did you think? Are you grossed out?" Davede grinned at her.

She shook her head. "No, I mean, it was strange and kind of macabre, what with the blood drinking and the jug of ancestral blood, and all, but it also seemed very sacred and beautiful."

Davede gulped and nodded. His eyes looked a little moist, and Piper wondered if he was imagining his own mating ceremony. She knew she was. She might not be ready just yet, but someday she would.

She gave him a smile and a look that hopefully he would see as a promise for the future. He must have, because he leaned in and kissed her like she belonged to him.

"What happens now?" She whispered, breathless, once he pulled away. She expected him to propose to her or say something dramatic. She tensed, worried that he'd think she was ready now, but instead he smiled and said, "Now we all get drunk and party all night."

Piper let our a relieved laugh. "Now that sounds like a wedding."

CHAPTER TWENTY-THREE

When the crowd let loose at the end of the ceremony, Caroline's body shook as the tension drained out of her. She'd done it! She'd made a public, lifetime commitment to a vampire, been initiated into their society, and survived her first, official vampire event.

She needed a drink, or a nap, or better yet, she needed to curl up in bed with Roric and finish their mating. The ceremony was important, but they weren't really mated until they had a complete blood exchange. It sounded scary, but Roric promised her it was the most incredible thing ever. At least, that was what he'd been told.

Roric took her hand and led her off the platform and back down the tunnel to the room where they'd waited for the ceremony to begin. He turned to her and slowly unzipped her robe like he was anticipating that she'd be naked underneath. Instead, she wore a gorgeous gown with yards of red satin that fell to the floor in a round bell around her legs.

Roric let the robe drop to the floor then slid his hands down her bare, goose-pimpled arms. He swallowed hard as he let his eyes rove down her body slowly then back up to latch onto her eyes. His own tiger's eye jewels sparkled with love and excitement. "You look so gorgeous in this."

With shaking fingers, Caroline unzipped his robe, revealing a sharp, black suit with a starched, white dress shirt and a red tie. She ran her hands down the thick, high-end fabric of his shirt, appreciating it, but wishing she could touch the skin and muscles underneath. By the look in his eyes, Roric felt the same way about her.

"Do we really have to go back out there? Can't we sneak out the back, or something?"

He chuckled, a deep, throaty sound that went straight to her groin. "Sorry, no dice. Our adoring fans await."

"You mean your adoring fans," she grumbled. Roric, while previously held in high regard because of his family and position, had been elevated to hero status after the bombing that took out the majority of the rogues. He and Taven had both been honored by the Modesa police department and given symbolic keys to the city.

There would probably always be rogues to catch, but the one's who'd instigated the rebellion were all gone. The school had reopened, and any unregistered vampires were enrolled and put through a three-month assimilation program. They'd tightened up the laws, too, so any vampire who was caught in a crime got a much harsher sentence. Things had settled down a lot, so Roric was free to spend more time with Caroline without feeling guilty about it.

Roric cupped her cheek in his hand and stroked the skin with his thumb. "You have fans, too, you know."

She cringed, well aware of her new fame. When the story got out about her ordeal, humans and vampires all over had been impressed by her bravery. Of course, the media had dug into her past and unearthed the story about her parents' death, too. The fact that she'd overcome her fear and hatred of vampires, accepted her new life as one of them, and fallen in love with her rescuer had everyone swooning. She'd become a media darling and the new face of the modern vampire.

She didn't really like all the attention, but her story seemed to give credence to the idea that even illegally-turned vampires could be trusted and helped to repair the public image of vampires after the rebellion. She supposed she could sacrifice some privacy for the sake of the cause.

She had also resumed her support group meetings for newly-turned vampires at the school, under the watchful eye of some highly-trained volunteers who made sure everyone stayed safe. She felt like she was doing her part to help people who went through the same thing she did.

"I'm your biggest fan, though." Roric pulled her closer then leaned in and kissed her. His lips sent tingles of pleasure coursing through her veins, igniting every inch of her skin. She quivered and sucked at his lips and tongue, eager to devour him. When she accidentally nicked his lip with her fang, Roric pulled away.

"Umm, we better stop while we still can. You ready to go greet our guests?"

Caroline groaned. "I suppose so."

He took her hand and led her back out to the main cavern where the party was already in full swing. Romantic music echoed off the walls of the chamber, and alcohol flowed freely from the portable bar they'd brought in for the occasion. Another table was serving fancy hors d'oeuvres.

Roric guided Caroline to the bar for some liquid courage. Her coworker, Gray, stood behind the bar grinning widely. She'd invited him to the ceremony as a guest, but when he found out she was going to have a bar, he insisted she let him tend it. He said he wanted to make sure she had the best bar service, but she suspected he just wanted an excuse to chat up all the single vampires.

"Hey girl, congratulations! You did awesome up there. I have to say, that ceremony was some freaky stuff, though." Gray reached across the bar to hug her then shook hands with Roric.

She had to admit, the ceremony was strange, but no stranger than the fact that she had just gotten mated to a vampire. She still could hardly believe the twists her life had taken in the last several months. But the most important thing was, she was happy. And she had an eternity to enjoy her new life with Roric. She supposed she better get used to socializing with the vampire community. She was going to be part of it for a long time.

She gave Gray a wry smile. "I think I need a bourbon."

Her poured the drink and handed it to her and she quickly downed it in one gulp.

"Damn, girl. You want another?"

She nodded and held out her glass for a refill. Gray filled it up again, but she didn't down that one, just took a few sips. "So, did you meet anyone interesting yet?"

Gray grinned and wiggled his eyebrows. "That was nice how they had the single vamps standing in the back for the ceremony. Very convenient. Made it easy to know who to look for later."

Caroline laughed. Like always, Gray had a way of

214

relaxing her. "I'm sure that's why they did it that way. See any good prospects?"

"I've got my eye on a few. Maybe Roric can help me out. Does the guy in the purple tie bat for my team?" Gray pointed at a vampire.

Roric rolled his eyes and shook his head at Gray, and Caroline turned to look out at the crowd. Her liquor-infused confidence took a hit. Every single person in the room would want to talk to her. She held up the bourbon and looked at the crowd through the glass. It didn't look any less intimidating through the amber liquid. Sighing, she chugged the second drink, too, then smacked the empty glass down on the bar.

"Okay, let's do this. The sooner we get started, the sooner we can go home." Caroline stomped out into the crowd, and Roric scurried after her.

It took almost three hours for them to greet everyone, thank them for their congratulating remarks, and have the same polite conversations a hundred times. By the time they'd acknowledged the last guest, Caroline was hungry, grumpy, and bloodthirsty. She grabbed Roric's arm, her fake smile so tight on her face she couldn't break it. "Take me home now, or I'm going home with the first vampire who will."

Roric gave her that sexy grin that always made her feel a little woozy. "Yes, ma'am. Wouldn't want you backing out on me before we sealed the deal."

He took her hand and guided her around the outskirts of the crowd so they were less likely to be stopped by chatty well-wishers. As soon as they stepped into the tunnel that led to the outside, Caroline let out a deep sigh.

He put an arm over her shoulder and pulled her into his

side. "You did great, Caroline. I couldn't be more proud of you."

"I'm proud of you, too, Roric. I couldn't be prouder to be mated to you." Roric was everything she could ever hope for in a mate, and she didn't regret any of the trials that had brought her to him. She shook her head, amazed at how far she'd come. From despising vampires to binding herself to one for all eternity. What a wild ride.

The ride home was just as intense as Roric broke every traffic law to get them home as soon as possible. They made it there in half the time it should've taken. Roric peeled into the driveway and slammed the brakes on, making the car shudder in protest, when he got to the parking area in the back of the house. Quick as a flash, he was beside her door. He scooped her up and carried her into the mansion.

Just like the first time he'd brought her there, he carried her up to his suite and laid her out on his bed, only this time she was wide awake and there was no question about what was going to happen. Caroline gave him a happy grin. "The zipper is on the back of this dress."

"I know, it's been teasing me all night, begging me to pull it down. I don't think I'll give it the satisfaction." Roric grabbed the top of her dress and yanked it down, tearing the fine satin off her body. Caroline yelped then started giggling.

Roric ripped off his own clothes, too, mindless of the expensive, new suit. Then he launched himself at her, making the bed bounce as he landed on top of her, only his bent elbows keeping him from crushing her. The move only made her laugh more, but Roric wasn't having it.

He smashed his lips against hers, silencing her, then

devoured her mouth with his till she groaned. Caroline wiggled her arms free and wrapped them around his torso, scratching her nails down his back then squeezing the firm, round muscles below it. He squirmed against her, digging his erection into her, making her crave more.

Then he moved his attention to her neck, kissing, and sucking, and nipping at the skin, but not hard enough to draw blood. Her body writhed underneath his, desperate for his touch. She lifted her head to his neck, eager to sink her teeth into him, but as soon as she got close, he moved down to her breast.

He sucked greedily at the taut nipple then rolled it around between his teeth like he was going to bite down. Caroline gasped, and her chest curved up to meet him. But he didn't give her what she wanted. Instead, he kissed a trail down her abdomen, setting a kaleidoscope of butterflies loose in her belly. They rushed though her body, tickling every nerve.

Then his lips followed the curve of her hip around to her thigh. He pushed her legs apart, exposing the tender, inner flesh. He ran his thumbs down the crease at the top of each leg. Caroline squirmed at his touch. Normally, she appreciated his tantalizing caresses, but today she had no patience for them.

"I can't wait any longer, Roric, please."

Roric dropped his head and sank his fangs into her inner thigh then began to drink from her, sucking her blood from her in deep, greedy pulls. She cried out and convulsed as pleasure ripped through her body. It felt incredible, but it wasn't what she wanted.

She only let him drink for a few moments before she dug her nails into his arms and pulled him back up her body till his face was hovering over hers. Neither one of them said anything for a long moment as they stared at each other. She could look into his eyes forever, lost in the mesmerizing pattern of amber, gold, and brown.

She saw every good thing about him in those eyes. He had never been a human like she had, but his eyes reflected more humanity than many humans she knew. In his eyes, she saw kindness, compassion, devotion, and most of all, love.

"I love you, Roric. Will you mate with me?"

"I thought you'd never ask." He plunged his fangs into her neck then and buried his hard length inside her. She cried out at the invasion, but quickly sank into the pleasure. It washed through her body in wave after wave as he alternated between sucking and thrusting.

When she had the energy, she lifted her head and bit into his neck, latching onto him. Blood gushed into her desiccated mouth, soothing her need. The pleasure swelled to ecstasy as she drew mouthfuls of blood from deep within his veins. The hot, metallic liquid coated her tongue and throat and filled her body with a warm heaviness. She glutted herself on it.

Roric kept up a slow but constant rhythm, keeping pace with their drinking. As her pleasure built higher and higher, she felt her body weakening from loss of blood. Roric was draining her dry. But she was draining him, too, and his blood filled her belly.

Finally, with one last hard stroke and suck, she came undone. Roric climaxed into her, and her body convulsed as an orgasm took over her, shattering her. Roric collapsed on top of her. She cried out his name and clutched at him with weak, lifeless limbs as the world around her dissolved into blackness.

Slowly, the blood in her belly seeped into her veins, taking the place of the blood she'd lost. Eventually, her body fluttered back to life, but she felt the difference immediately. Roric wasn't just on top of her, inside of her; now he was part of her. She felt his lifeblood pumping through her veins with every heartbeat. She couldn't tell where she ended and he started. They were one, and nothing had ever felt more right to her.

The End.

Check out these other great books by Kellie:

About the Author

Kellie McAllen is a USA Today bestselling author who has her nose in a book whenever she can. When she's not reading or writing, she also likes to guest judge on DWTS (from her living room), watch cat videos, and eat too much pizza and chocolate.

Keep up with Kellie at:
www.kelliemcallen.com

Join Kellie's mailing list to be notified when new releases are available.
You'll also receive access to FREE BONUS SCENES!
http://bit.ly/bonus_scenes

Made in the USA
Columbia, SC
15 November 2018